This beautiful young woman wasn't in the least what he wanted as a governess.

He had to be mad. Yet Carrie's light fragrance filled the interior of the car with such images of spring blossom and sweet breezes.

Carrie glanced out of the window. "My stepmother is under the impression you and I are having a secret affair."

"So what did you tell her?"

"Only that you were a friend. That you were divorced and you have a little girl."

"Nothing about coming back with me to Maramba?"

She was shocked by the effect of his words on her. "I wasn't totally sure you wanted me," she confessed.

"You really want this job?"

"At the moment I desperately need it," she admitted frankly.

W9-AUI-114

Margaret Way takes great pleasure in her work and works hard at her pleasure. She enjoys tearing off to the beach with her family at weekends, loves haunting galleries and auctions and is completely given over to French champagne "for every possible joyous occasion." She was born and educated in the river city of Brisbane, Australia, and now lives within sight and sound of beautiful Moreton Bay.

Books by Margaret Way

HARLEQUIN ROMANCE®

MARGARET WAY
Master of Maramba

THE AUSTRALIANS

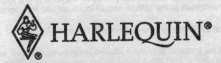
HARLEQUIN®

TORONTO • NEW YORK • LONDON
AMSTERDAM • PARIS • SYDNEY • HAMBURG
STOCKHOLM • ATHENS • TOKYO • MILAN • MADRID
PRAGUE • WARSAW • BUDAPEST • AUCKLAND

ISBN 0-373-03671-X

MASTER OF MARAMBA

First North American Publication 2001.

CHAPTER ONE

SHE didn't see the car until it purred right up to her. A big opulent Jaguar. Platinum. This year's colour. Only seconds before she had scanned the jacaranda-lined street: traffic moving at a clip along the terrace, nothing in this narrow side street where she always tried to park when visiting her favourite uncle, in fact her only uncle. James Halliday of Halliday, Scholes & Associates, solicitors and tax advisers to the seriously rich. The busy professional area which included architects, engineers, town planners, and two very trendy but non-flashy interior designers, was fully parked except for the spot she'd had the great good fortune to drive into as another driver moved out. There was a space of sorts behind her suitable for a pokey little car like her own. She'd tried that in the past with the rear end showing the scars. No way could the driver of the magnificent Jag, she could see it was a man, squeeze into the spot. The thought gave her a certain perverse satisfaction.

Carrie locked her car, hoping the Jaguar would glide past, instead the occupant drove alongside, coming so close she could feel the familiar agitation start up inside her. She flattened her whole body against the side of her own car watching in sick fascination as the driver turned his coal-black head over his shoulder preparatory to putting the limousine into reverse.

The usual male derring-do. This one had more than his share.

No way could he miss hitting the trunk of the jacaranda tree unless he knew the exact dimensions of the Jag and the spot down to the last millimetre. She knew she was staring after him, her upper body now slumped sideways giving every appearance of a woman who had narrowly missed being run over. She didn't know whether to laugh or cry. She only knew she couldn't control her reactions. Ever since her accident she'd lost her emotional equanimity becoming almost a stranger to herself, fearful, wary, her nerves running on overdrive.

While she awaited the ker-uuun-ch the driver confounded her by manoeuvring that great big car into that teeny little space, startling her into unwilling admiration. But it happened sometimes. Especially with men. Even the total idiots among them seemed to know exactly how to reverse park. Had it been another woman she would have burst into applause but no such luck for his lordship.

Carrie looked away, pretending utter indifference. Her heartbeats had quietened now she was free to go about her business, realising at the last minute she'd forgotten her sunglasses and the spring sunshine was dazzling. Shafts of it flashed through the lacy canopy of the trees. Another month and they would be out in glorious lavender-blue flower, an event the whole subtropical city of Brisbane looked forward to. Except maybe the students. Jacaranda time. Exam time. She knew all about that. An honours graduate from the Conservatorium of Music. Winner of the Gold Medal for outstanding achievement. Winner of the National Young Performers' Award for her playing of the Rachmaninoff 2nd Piano Concerto. Accepted into the prestigious Julliard Academy in New York. A young woman with a very bright future.

Until the accident.

With an unhappy shrug, Carrie opened the door, reached in, and picked up the glasses, before giving the door a good healthy slam to work off excess energy, panic, irrational hostility, whatever. She'd have a lifetime to come to terms with her broken dreams. A whole world opened to her. Now shut.

She turned, watching the man get out of the car. He was looking straight at her, something questioning in his expression as though he saw things going on in her face. Or her *heart*. The thought shook her. She had instant impressions of her own. Dark-haired, dark-eyed, dark tanned skin but with a healthy glow. As tall as Mount Everest and just as impressive. Very likely a huge source of income. An aura like that only came with tons of money. But he wasn't deskbound. Too powerful. Hard muscles rippled beneath his beautiful, elegant city clothes. The walk was purposeful, athletic, the action as superlative as the powerful cylinders of the Jag. If a halo of light had surrounded him she wouldn't have been a bit surprised. The tan hadn't come from lying around on the beach, either. He put her more in mind of some godlike explorer gazing off into sun-scorched infinity. The Red Centre. The Dead Heart. She particularly liked that image. It seemed to suit him yet she stared back as though he were transparent. She had to find someone to hate today. He was it. Mr. Heartbreak, Mr. Trouble, Mr. Larger than Life. Men who irradiated their surroundings always were.

"Have a problem?"

Like the rest of him his voice riveted her attention. Overly authoritative from where she was coming from. Super-confident, super-resonant, dark in colour. A man of substance and it showed. She assumed he was the boss of a huge corporation. A guy who gave orders all day while other people jumped. Not her. She prided herself on kowtowing to no one, though her body carried the odd conviction something significant was happening to her. Why was he looking at her like that? She was feeling the impact right through her body.

Yet she answered coolly giving off her own aura. "Not

in the least. I share your enthusiasm for parking in cramped spaces. Only I didn't think you could make it.''

''Why not? It wasn't difficult.''

He sounded amused. Carrie watched him approach her, billowing that male aura. He stopped just before it completely enveloped her. Above-average height for a woman he made her feel like a doll with a slight case of hysteria. It was way too humbling. And it stiffened her backbone.

His brilliant eyes—how could black eyes be filled with such light?—continued to sweep her, missing absolutely nothing including the tiny heart-shaped beauty spot above the swell of her right breast.

''I had the decided impression you thought you were about to be run over?''

''What, on the basis of a raised eyebrow?'' she parried.

''Actually you appeared to crumple. You couldn't really have been frightened. *Were* you?''

''Of course not.'' She tasted a faint bitterness at the back of her throat.

''I'm glad,'' he answered. ''You were in absolutely no danger. Perhaps you have a thing about male drivers.'' He answered mildly, she considered. For him. ''Pretty much all of us can park better than our womenfolk. Your left rear tyre is rammed into the gutter by the way.''

Carrie didn't give him the satisfaction of turning to look. ''I'm not one of the world's greatest parkers I admit.'' She made it sound as if one only needed to be if one drove an armoured truck.

''That's perfectly clear,'' the vibrant voice lightly mocked. ''Be assured I'm not sore at you.''

''I didn't imagine you were.''

''Then confess. Why so nervous? I'm almost positive you're nervous. *Why?* It's broad daylight. I don't normally make women uneasy.''

"Are you sure?" He couldn't fail to hear the astonished irony in her tone.

"It's obvious you don't know me." The jet-black eyes glinted over her as though no one *but no one* spoke to him this way. "Look there's no traffic," he pointed out in an unexpectedly gentle voice, glancing up and down the street. "Would you like me to escort you to the other side?"

And let him touch her? This dominating man. She didn't dare. She held up her two palms, then dropped them in one graceful gesture.

"Surely you jest?" She spoke sweetly when she could cheerfully have pushed him over. An enormous not to say impossible job.

"I jest not." His mouth was handsome, sensual in cut, but very firmly held. "You on the other hand seem to be kneading the hem of your skirt."

She glanced down. She was, too. Another nervous habit. "All right, if you must know I thought you came much too close to me."

"You should talk to somebody about it."

"About what?" Colour whipped into her cheeks, antagonism into her tone.

"I suppose the best word would be phobia." He looked squarely at her.

It was a big mistake to have spoken to him at all. "You're saying *I* have a phobia?" She gave him what she thought of as her dagger look. "That's a bit much for a complete stranger?"

He seemed mightily unimpressed, shrugging a nonchalant broad shoulder. "Seems very much like it to me."

That was the final straw. To be caught out. So easily. By a stranger. Carrie turned away so tempestuously her thick silky amber hair whipped around her like a pennant in a sea breeze. "Have a nice day," she clipped off.

"You, too." He sketched a brief salute, watching her stalk away, on her beautiful long legs. Sort of angry. And it showed. She was muttering something to herself as she went.

Then abruptly she turned, like a woman determined on having the last word. Point of honour. He almost laughed aloud.

"I hope you're not planning on parking there too long?" she threw at him with that rather tantalising hauteur. "An inspector might just wander by. It's not actually a parking space, you know. I should warn you. I might be forced to back into you in order to get out. You've virtually jammed me in."

"Not at all."

He moved with dark energy to double-check, giving her a sudden smile that did strange things to her. Formidable in height and demeanour—his employees probably addressed him staring at his feet—that smile was extraordinary, making nerves twitch all over her skin.

"Anyway I'm not worried," he pronounced casually. "Just leave your name and address under the wiper should anything go wrong."

"I'll try very hard to see it doesn't."

How could he be enjoying this? he thought. He almost never got into conversations with strange young women. And this one was not only hostile, but intriguingly familiar. A firehead to match her rare colouring. Hair like a good sherry with the light glinting through it. Beautiful clear skin with an apricot blush. Golden-brown eyes, almost a topaz. Her hadn't seen a woman with such clarity for years. And she was just a kid. She carried the beautiful scent of youth with her. Probably ten or more years his junior. He would be thirty-two his next birthday. A thirty-two-year-old divorcee with a child, Regina. He cared about her deeply. But the devastating fact was Regina wasn't his child. She was the result of one of Sharon's affairs. Funny the young woman who was stalking away from him had put all thought of Sharon out of his mind.

"Take care!" he called after her. "You city girls are so damned aggressive."

Carrie despite her avowed intention found herself stopping. Wasn't that strange. *City girls.* "So where do you hail from?" she challenged, wondering what imp of mischief had taken possession of her. He was Someone. She was sure of it.

"A long way from here," he drawled.

"And here was I thinking you're the sort of man who *always* knows what to expect."

"Careful," he said. "I might be still here when you get back."

Carrie waved a backward hand as though everything he said was of no real importance. She supposed she was being very rude but crossing swords with that man had helped to bring a little pleasure into her blighted young life. She'd never had an experience quite like that. But then as far as she knew, he hadn't, either. Maybe he would be there when she returned. The little flurry of excitement made her furious at herself.

James Halliday's secretary announced her arrival like an aide might announce a candidate for a court investiture, Carrie thought. She'd known Ms. Galbally since she was a little girl but the secretary had never once veered from the very formal. As a child and adolescent she'd always been Catrina, not Carrie. Once she turned eighteen she became Miss Russell. Ms. Galbally was a middle-aged saturine woman of handsome appearance and Carrie knew other people found her intimidating, but according to her uncle she was just about "perfect." So much for appearances, Carrie thought trying but not succeeding in looking honoured.

"Carrie, sweetheart!" Her uncle himself opened the door, handsome, genial, charming, fifty and looking nothing like it, four years older than her late mother but very much like her in appearance which was to say like herself, ushering her into an office as big as Central station but cosy as a den. It had a great view over the river; the walls were mahogany-panelled, lined with deep antique bookcases holding leather-bound legal tomes, a series of excellent quite valuable architectural drawings took up the rest of the wall space along with a few striking oil paintings, seascapes in gilt frames. James Halliday was a well-known yachtsman.

A magnificent Persian rug, all wonderful dark blues and rich rubies adorned the discreetly carpeted floor. Glass display cabinets set off a few choice pieces of James Halliday's collection of Ming dynasty Chinese porcelain, heralding the fact James Halliday was a collector, as well. An enormous partner's desk held centre court with a splendid high-backed chair ranged behind it. It was abundantly clear her uncle was doing very well. But not as well as her father who owned a large city electrical firm.

The two men did not get on. Different personalities; different interests; different callings. Carrie loved both of them but from her mother's side of the family she had inherited a great love of the "arts," a sphere that held little interest for her father, her stepmother Glenda and her stepsister, Melissa, three years her junior.

"Like some coffee, darling?" James Halliday asked, looking at his niece searchingly but with great affection. She had suffered a devastating blow and in many ways it showed. Her characteristic sparkle had banked down but he knew in his heart she had the inner resources to pull through this major setback to her life's plans.

Carrie sank into a plush, leather-upholstered armchair, sighing gently. "I'd love it. No one drinks coffee at home anymore," she added after James put through his request. "Glenda has convinced Dad it's bad for him. Bad for everyone. She doesn't like my buying it, either. I'll have to move out. It was always going to happen. Now I'm not going to New York, the sooner the better. Dad won't be happy but he's not around much to know just how things are between us."

"It's the greatest pity you and Melissa aren't close," James mourned.

"Isn't it? Glenda's fault, I'm sure. Mel would never have felt the way she does if Glenda hadn't stirred up such feelings of jealousy."

"I know your stepmother has made life difficult for you." James confined himself to a single remark when he wanted to say lots more.

"She never wanted me, Jamie. She didn't want a ready-made child who just happened to be the image of her husband's first wife. I swear to this day she's jealous of my mother."

James nodded his agreement. He'd seen too many upsetting signs of it. "She can't help it. It's her nature. We both know, too, she's deeply resented your talent. All the attention you got because of it, prizes and awards. It singled you out."

"And not Mel. Still, she doesn't have to worry now," Carrie said wryly.

"You're still a highly accomplished pianist," her uncle reminded her, himself devastated by the crushing results of her accident.

"It doesn't seem like much of a compensation. To think I had to be involved in a car crash the very day I got news I'd been accepted into the Julliard. Fate taking a nasty turn."

"It was a tragedy, sweetheart, but you can't let it ruin your life," James warned. "You need time to recover, then you have to pick up the pieces. It could have been very much worse than broken ribs and a crushed little finger."

"That won't stand up to the rigours of a career. I know. I'm trying, Jamie. Really I am, but it's hard. The funny part is, Dad is sad for me but he's relieved, too. He didn't want me going off overseas. He wants me at home. Safely married. He wants grandchildren in time."

He wants. He wants, James thought. He'd wanted my beautiful sister but never made her happy. Trying to confine her fine spirit as he had never succeeded with his daughter.

"Your father has many good qualities but he isn't musical."

"You mean he hasn't got a musical bone in his body." Carrie gave a broken laugh. "Dad has always been proud of me but he can't come close to the music I play. *Played*. I haven't touched the piano since the accident."

"Nearly a year ago."

"No time at all."

"I agree." James couldn't meet her glistening topaz eyes. "Not for your heartache and bitter disappointment, to heal."

"I don't enjoy teaching, Jamie. I suppose I was too much of a performer."

"And you're so *young*," James returned. "Twenty-two is no age at all."

"Old enough to move out," Carrie retorted. "I'd have done it before today only I didn't want to hurt Dad. Glenda is *never* going to like me. We can't be friends."

James snorted in disgust. "I don't want to be unkind but Melissa is very much like her mother or she's rapidly becoming that way. I think a shift might be best for all. Where would you like to go? You know you can come to

Liz and me. We'd love to have you. Not blessed with children of our own, you've been everything to us."

"And you've been wonderful to me. Liz has been far more of a mother figure than Glenda could ever have hoped to be, but it's time I struck out on my own, Jamie. You know I'm right."

"Your father would buy you an apartment, surely? He's a wealthy man."

"I'm not going to ask him, Jamie. Glenda would bitterly resent that. I bought my own car. I'll rent my own flat."

Protective James didn't like the sound of that at all. "What about if I bought you one? I can afford it. Of course I wouldn't like to go against your father. Add to the…" He almost said, chip on his shoulder.

"List of resentments," Carrie supplied. "Bless you for everything, Jamie, but I'm ready and able to stand on my own two feet. Lord knows I spent long enough as a student. I suppose I should undertake a doctorate. I may not be able to make the grade as a concert artist but music has been my life. I worked so hard. All those years of practice! I guess I'm stuck with a teaching career so I'll need all the qualifications I can get."

"Agreed. But how can you support yourself if you won't allow help?" There was worry in Jamie's voice. "Part-time work won't be enough. Lessons here and there."

"I still have Grandma's money." Carrie referred to her inheritance from her maternal grandmother who had pined away from grief at the loss of Carrie's mother, her only daughter. "It'll see me through. The thing is, Jamie, I want to get away. I need to find a bolthole. At least for a while. I have to get away from the whole music scene until I can come to terms with what has happened to me."

There was deep feeling in her uncle's answering tone. "I can understand that, darling. The funny thing is I have a client, our most valuable client I should add, who's looking for a governess for his little daughter. Not that you're governess material,'' he quickly considered.

"Who said?"

"Sweetheart.'' James gave a fond laugh. "You're not. Take it from me. You're so gifted. So beautiful. A young woman to show off not hide in the wilds.''

"The wilds?'' Carrie's arched brows shot up. "Tell me more.'' She fought down a very sharp ache inside.

"I'm sorry I started this,'' James paused as a tap came on his door. A young female office worker entered wheeling a trolley set with what looked like a mini-banquet. James Halliday had a sweet tooth but showed not an extra ounce for it.

"Over there, thanks, Ann.'' He gave the girl his charming smile. "Looks good.''

"All lovely and fresh, Mr. Halliday,'' Ann smiled, turning her pretty face to Carrie who returned her pleasant greeting.

"How you don't get fat!'' Carrie wondered affectionately, after Ann had departed. "Just as well you have your sailing.'' She got up from her chair to pour.

"I'm going out on the bay this weekend. Want to come?''

"Yes, please!'' Carrie's golden-brown eyes brightened. She loved boats. Loved the water. She had sailed with her uncle since she was a child right up to the Whitsundays in the glorious Great Barrier Reef.

When they were both seated, coffee in hand, three delicious little pastries to James' left, Carrie picked up where he had left off. "I take it the governess job is on an Outback property.''

"Property doesn't say it, love.'' James stirred his coffee with vigour. "More like a private kingdom. The family are big operators. They control over four million hectares spread across ten stations around the state. My client is one of the nation's largest private land barons. Queensland remains home to the country's biggest cattle kings, as you know.''

"So we're talking the Channel Country in the far south-west,'' Carrie concluded. ''Couldn't get farther away.'' Well over a thousand miles.

''No.'' James shook his thickly thatched head. ''The chain does extend to the Cattle Country but the family base is in North Queensland. It's the linchpin in the whole operation. Not their biggest holding but perhaps the best. A marine flood plain that provides pretty well constant lush green feed. Cattle from all over their holdings can be fattened there. It's a Brahmin stud.''

''Called?'' Carrie savoured her coffee. As usual it was very good.

''Maramba Downs. Maramba.''

''I'm sure I've heard of it.''

''Very likely,'' James answered complacently selecting a mouth-watering patty. ''Royce is often in the news.''

''Royce who? Come on, you're being very cagey.''

''Carrie, love, this job wouldn't suit you,'' James said, wondering why he had even mentioned it.

''The fact is I'm becoming more interested by the minute.''

''It's not going to happen. I understand the little girl is…difficult. Other governesses haven't lasted long.''

''What does the little terror do?'' Carrie asked, having a special soft spot for ''little terrors.'' She had been one herself.

James laughed. ''I know what you're thinking. Didn't Glenda complain a lot about you? Royce sees it differently of course. The *governesses* are at fault.''

''Aaaaah! Does the dragon have a surname?''

''Royce McQuillan. Splendid fellow. One of the finest

young men I've ever met. Hasn't had an easy life, either. He lost his father and mother a few years back. They were killed in a plane crash holidaying overseas. Then his marriage broke up.''

''Oh, dear!'' Carrie slumped, knowing what heartache meant. ''The mother didn't take the child? That's unusual.''

''Didn't want her, it appears.'' James' kind eyes grew soulful. ''I don't know the full story in that area, Royce doesn't explain much. You'd have to know of *her,* though she'd be some years older than you. Thirty, maybe thirty-one. Very glamorous woman. Almost a beauty but too brittle. Sharon Rowlands, that was. Hugh Rowlands heads the Standford Pastoral Company. Ruth Rowlands and her daughter spend most of their time following the social scene. You see them in all the magazines.''

''Except I've been too busy to read them. The little girl must have been devastated when her parents split up. How old is she?''

''A very precocious six going on seven,'' James said.

''So they were married young?'' Carrie observed, making calculations.

''According to Liz the marriage was arranged while they were both in the cradle.''

''That's how it works in some families. It didn't take them long to grow apart.''

''No.'' James truly, genuinely, felt very sorry for his client. ''Royce has very big responsibilities, big commitments. The talk is Sharon got bored.''

''Bored?'' Carrie was stunned. What sort of life did this Sharon want? ''So you've met her?''

''A few times,'' James said.

''What did you think of her as a person?''

''Too shallow for Royce. Liz thought so, too. She's an excellent judge of character.''

"Yes, she is." Carrie had turned very serious. "The mother must have a heart of stone if she could bear to leave her child."

James stared into his coffee cup. "I hate to say it but the word is the little one might interfere with her pleasure. I expect she'll remarry though Liz thinks she'll never get over Royce, let alone find another man like him."

"Maybe if she still cares about him they could get back together," Carrie said reasonably. "Make a go of it for their child. They can't have any of the financial worries that put a strain on most couples."

"Money doesn't ensure happiness, my darling," James said heavily, thinking of any number of his wealthy clients who had finished up in the divorce courts. "I thank God for my marriage every day of my life."

Carrie gave him the old warm smile. "You're beautiful people, Jamie. You and Liz. Beautiful, tolerant, generous, caring people." Determinedly she pushed all thought of her stepmother's mean-spiritedness from her mind. "I love you. Always will."

They sat quietly for a few minutes, the atmosphere full of an easy companionship. "You know I'm like your father in this respect," James confided after a while. "I couldn't bear the thought of your going away. I know you had to for your career. I was terror stricken when I got that phone call...." He broke off, the news of Carrie's accident embedded in his consciousness.

"I know, James. It could have been much worse." Carrie forced a smile.

"Much, much worse, my darling. Losing my sister was a terrible blow. I couldn't face anything horrible happening to you." James spoke huskily. "There's something else in store for you, kitten." He used an old pet name. "Something wonderful. It may not seem like it now."

"It doesn't." Carrie swallowed. "It's hard for me, Jamie. Very hard."

"Yes, yes." James reached over to grip his niece's left hand. "Liz and I understand what the loss of your career means to you."

"Of course. I may not have had a career." Carrie tried to look at it another way. "I mightn't have made the grade. There are many, many fine young pianists out there. One almost has to have a gimmick."

"Your beauty? Your personality?" James suggested, then stopped abruptly, realising it was all over.

"But I don't need a gimmick after all." For a moment Carrie had a stark image of the crash. Horror then sudden darkness. Then the full realisation when she woke up in hospital. "I need a job, Jamie," she said. "You can help me. You're handling this matter for your client?"

"I was going to allow Galbally to conduct the interviews," James said.

Carrie allowed herself a little gasp of dismay not lost on her uncle.

"Dearest, *I* don't have time," James explained. "Women are so much better at these things."

"Not Ms. Galbally." Carrie raised her eyebrows.

"She takes her responsibilities very seriously," James said loyally.

"I'm sure she does. Can't *you* recommend me, Jamie?"

James dropped his head forward. "Your father wouldn't like it at all. I can just image his response."

"Glenda would."

James responded to the irony. "But it mightn't work out at all, Carrie. I don't want to put you into a situation where you might be unhappy. Cut off and depressed."

"Unhappier, don't you mean? I can look after a little girl. She must be especially vulnerable. Like me. Maybe I can bring something to her. Two female creatures under pressure.''

James nibbled his nether lip. "Royce is coming to the office in a half hour. We have business to attend to. The revival in beef prices has boosted sales in the rural property sector. He's thinking in terms of expansion.''

"Does he want to own the whole country?'' Carrie asked with mild sarcasm.

"We need men like Royce McQuillan, dearest.''

"I know,'' she relented. "Would it be okay if I waited?''

James sat back, focusing totally on his niece. "You're serious about this?''

"Yes.'' She touched the little finger of her right hand, and rubbed it in a distracted fashion. Strange, it still *looked* okay. "Of course I won't know how serious until I lay eyes on the great nation builder, but as you like and approve of him he must be okay.''

"Indeed he is, which is not say he's an *easy* man,'' James considered. "He's only into his thirties but already he has extraordinary presence. Such an aura! It takes most men years of achievement to acquire that.''

"Must be all the money,'' Carrie quipped dryly.

James nodded. "That helps. The break-up of his marriage changed him in significant ways. Less likely to relax. Let down his guard. He's more formidable.''

"He sounds an uncomfortable person. Is he bitter?''

James pursed his lips. "Not bitter as in surly or unpleasant. Nothing like that. He has great charm when he cares to use it. But the marriage break-up took away a certain lightness of spirit. The capacity for easy laughs.''

"Made him more wary of women I expect?''

"*Beautiful* women.'' James looked full at her, captivated as ever by the lovely classical features, the bright colouring, most of all the close resemblance to his much-loved sister, Caroline.

That same lovely face now fell. "You mean he's looking for someone very *plain?*" The idea was unsettling.

"I think *pleasant* would be his choice." James glanced off.

"Then pleasant I'll be," said Carrie, all of a sudden sure life on an Outback cattle station would solve her problem.

She was holding the fort for Debra, Halliday, Scholes & Associates' receptionist when he came through the door, confounding her. The blood drummed in her ears. The world tilted again.

"Why, hello there." He spoke very smoothly as she looked up. "This is just *so* unexpected."

Somehow mercifully the moment passed. She was able to breathe again. "It is…odd," Carrie agreed, aware those brilliant black eyes were filled with amusement and mockery. "May I help you?" She was rather proud of the calm detachment of her voice.

"It's your boss I'm after. James Halliday."

"You have an appointment?" It couldn't be. It *couldn't* be.

"Of course I have an appointment." He gave a brief laugh. "You must be new. Royce McQuillan."

She was struck by dread. There goes the job. The bolt-hole. "Of course, Mr. McQuillan." She stared back at him. "The receptionist will be back in a moment but I'll ring through for you."

"No matter!" He dismissed that with a slight impatient gesture of his hand. "I'll go along. Mr. Halliday is expecting me."

"Then allow me to take you," Carrie offered, coming around the reception desk as Debra approached from the opposite direction, increasing her pace as she recognised the client.

"Good morning, Mr. McQuillan," she carolled, packing a lot of feeling into her voice. "Or is it afternoon?"

"In a few minutes." He glanced down at his watch. "How are you, Debra?"

"I'm well. And you?" The receptionist came to a halt, staring up into his face, obviously thrilled he had taken the time to say a few words to her.

"Fine." There was a brief glimpse of his devastating smile. Very white against the dark tan. "Busy as usual. This young lady here," he turned to Carrie now standing at his shoulder, "is going to escort me to Mr. Halliday's office."

"That's nice of you, Carrie," Debra said, her colour warm, eyes bright. "Carrie is…"

"In the office for the day." Carrie cut the other girl off smoothly. She didn't want her relationship to James explained quite yet.

Debra smiled touching a hand to her soft bubbly curls. "Nice to see you, Mr. McQuillan. I won't be here when you get back. I'll be going off for lunch."

"Joining the madding crowd?" He gave her a little salute.

"What part do you play in the scheme of things?" he asked Carrie as they moved off. "I recognise you from somewhere and I don't mean our previous encounter."

"I'm not famous," she said. It came off her tongue rather acidly.

"Is *that* what's tearing you apart?" He glanced down at her from his arrogant height.

"You're wrong. Believe me." Carrie kept on walking, slightly intimidated by his long stride.

"I don't think so."

Little flames glowed in the pupils of her eyes and she tilted her head. "You must spend your time trying to psychoanalyse people?"

"I haven't actually met anyone who acted quite like you," he returned blandly.

"I'm sure—absolutely sure—I don't understand you." She raised her delicate arched brows.

"Then I'll explain. In simple terms, you're *hostile*."

"You could very easily arouse those feelings in anybody." It slipped off her tongue before she could consider.

"For all I know you could be frightened of me?"

"Nonsense."

"Street terrorism?" the dark voice mocked.

"Have your bit of fun."

"Are you a lady lawyer?" He gave her his all-encompassing sidelong glance. "You don't look old enough, yet I'd say you're a match for most people."

"I'm not a lawyer." She turned to him sweetly. "I don't work for this firm."

"But you're somehow connected to James? I've finally figured it out." He paused so she was forced to pause, too. "I know he doesn't have a daughter. Come to think if it," he laughed suddenly as full comprehension set in. "There's quite a resemblance. You must be the niece. The brilliant young pianist?"

Except now I've been whittled down to size. "You *are* a detective," she said lightly. "Poirot on his best day."

"Why so snappy?" The striking face tautened as he stared down at her. "You have a wonderful future ahead of you, I understand?"

"An unfortunate part of my nature." They had turned into the top hallway, and now James Halliday himself emerged from his suite, anxious to greet such a valuable client personally.

"Royce," he cried with genuine pleasure, moving forward, hand outstretched. "Good to see you."

The two men shook hands.

"I see you've already met my niece?" James' smile widened to include the two of them.

"We haven't gotten around to formal introductions yet," Royce McQuillan drawled.

"Please allow me." Suddenly conscious of a certain tingle in the air, James performed the introductions, while Carrie, ashamed of the way she'd been acting and doing her utmost to avoid being overwhelmed, gave him her hand.

"*Catrina,* may I?" he asked.

"Everyone calls her Carrie." James smiled, extending an arm to usher them through the door.

She didn't have a clue what she was doing. She had never felt remotely like this around anyone else. The shooting sparks of electricity didn't stop even after he'd released her hand. She couldn't look at him. It was the dynamic aura, she consoled herself. Even James felt it and James was the complete man of the world.

A little later by the time they were inside James' office, she found her voice. "It's been a pleasure meeting you, Mr. McQuillan, but I should be on my way."

James' eyes found hers in perplexity. Something drastic must have happened to alter Carrie's plan. "But I thought, kitten…"

Carrie felt McQuillan's amusement. Kitten? How long since Jamie had called her kitten? Now twice in the one day. She turned to face Royce McQuillan square-on. "Goodbye."

She didn't offer the hand again but lifted a thick silky section of her hair from her collar as she spoke, tossing her head slightly to redistribute the mass.

An extraordinary alluring gesture, he thought. Kitten? She certainly had the colouring of a beautiful marmalade but this young woman had sharp claws. He noticed, too, the knuckles of her right hand were clenched white. They were beautiful hands. Long-fingered, strong-looking. A pianist's hands.

"I was rather hoping you'd stay and have lunch with us," he found himself saying. "My business with James won't take long."

"We're going to Oskars, sweetheart. You like it there." James weighed in, trying to encourage her. "They won't have any difficulty changing two places to three."

She wanted to go, unwillingly in thrall of him. "That's very nice of you, but…."

"Please, sit down both of you." James indicated the comfortable seating arrangement. "I was telling Carrie about your need of a governess for Regina," he said, turning his eyes in Carrie's direction.

"*Were* you? You can't have thought *she'd* be interested?" McQuillan returned suavely, waiting for Carrie to take a seat in the armchair opposite him, before sitting down.

It was time for Carrie to speak, James considered, or let the whole thing slide. Knowing her so well, he could see her moods, however, were fluctuating wildly.

"Actually I've been working so hard on my career I'm in need of a complete change."

Royce McQuillan stayed quiet for a moment wondering if she'd suffered some kind of nervous collapse. A burnout.

"I hardly see you as a governess," he said. "What do you know about the job?"

"Nothing!" Her amber eyes sparkled. "But I like children."

"Being able to handle them might matter more," he observed, his eyes touching on her slender body in a summery two-piece outfit of blouse and skirt, white with dark blue polka dots, the short skirt showing off her beautiful legs, the V-neck of the top revealing the slight cleft between her milk-white breasts. She had the flawless skin of certain redheads. Not a mark on it for all she lived in a subtropical climate.

Carrie bore his scrutiny by sitting very quietly. A kind of balancing act. "Who said I couldn't?" she retorted. "I've had quite a bit to do with talented children, coaching, giving lessons, master classes for the little ones."

"Regina is a child who likes getting her own way," he said matter-of-factly as though it needed to be said. "I don't know what James told you," McQuillan glanced in her uncle's direction, "but her mother left her in my sole custody. Regina isn't desolated but understandably she's found that difficult to handle."

As well she might, Carrie thought. Abandoned so early in life. This dizzyingly dynamic man for a father. "I had to live without my mother," she said quietly. "I've had a stepmother for most of my life."

"You don't like her?" he asked bluntly.

"There's no point in talking about it." Carrie shook her head, not wanting to be humiliated by this man any further. He didn't like her. She wasn't being terribly likeable. Under no circumstances would he employ her. She made to rise. "It was just an idea I had. A spur of the moment thing. Besides something about the story moved me. Regina's feelings that can't be dismissed and I need to help someone." To help myself, to survive, she thought but didn't say. "I'm sure Uncle James will find you someone you consider suitable, Mr. McQuillan." She stood up in one swift graceful movement. "I must decline your kind offer to have lunch. I have to see someone this afternoon at the Conservatorium." Easy to make it up.

He, too, stood up, his expression a little darker. "What a pity. I would have liked to get to know you better instead of a few snatched words. James has spoken of you often. I've just recalled where I saw you though I can see it has since disappeared.'' He turned to James. ''Remember that photograph of a little girl you used to have on your desk. It had a lovely antique silver frame.''

''Carrie, of course!'' James' face lit up. ''It's at home. Liz went off with it. She loves that one.''

''I was ten at the time.'' Carrie looked at Royce McQuillan in surprise.

''You haven't changed at all.''

''I have, too.'' I'm falling apart, Carrie thought, stunned how well she hid it. I just have to get away from this man.

''You're wonderfully observant, Royce,'' James said in his charming voice, fully conscious of the charge in the atmosphere.

''It's not a face one forgets.''

''No.'' James smiled at his niece, his heart in his eyes. ''Carrie is the image of her mother, my darling sister, Caroline. Having Carrie, Caro is always near.'' He reached out and slipped an arm around Carrie's waist, drawing her to him.

''Love you,'' she murmured, turning her head into her uncle's shoulder. ''Well, I must be off.'' Her voice picked up briskly. ''Enjoy your lunch.''

''Let's see, I take it you've withdrawn your candidature?'' Again Royce McQuillan cast his spell over her, his brilliant black gaze suggesting she was a highly volatile individual.

''I didn't think you liked me?'' she answered solemnly.

''Did I say so?''

''I believe you did. In certain ways.''

''Really?'' One black eyebrow shot up. ''I'm sorry you thought so. I didn't mean it in that way. If you *are* serious, perhaps we can discuss the matter again as you absolutely must rush off.'' It was obvious he hadn't believed in her excuse.

''When do you fly back home, Royce?'' James Halliday

asked, not quite sure what was going on. But something certainly was.

"Tomorrow."

His gaze held her as though she was pinned to the wall. "I think you want someone very different from me," Carrie said, suddenly anxious to back out of a dangerous situation while she could. This man could change her life. She knew it. And not for the better. She wasn't such a fool or so traumatized it hadn't struck her, though her reactions were multiple, the overriding one was sexual. The slightest contact with his hand had somehow compromised her. This man still had an ex-wife in the background. An ex-wife who wasn't over him yet. The mother of his child.

Carrie tilted her head to kiss her uncle's cheek. "See you, Jamie. Give my love to Liz."

"You are coming sailing with me?" James was mystified by her thoughts.

"Of course I am. Let's hope for a perfect weekend." Her skirt flaring as she changed direction, Carrie dared to glance in Royce McQuillan's direction. "I'm thinking how I'm going to get out of my parking spot. You're still there?"

"I don't know if I should let you do it," he said with a provocative stare.

"Do *what?* It would be nice if you'd let me in on this," James complained.

"I met Mr. McQuillan earlier on," Carrie explained. "We're both parked in the side street."

"I can come with you if you're worried," Royce McQuillan offered suavely. "Perhaps extricate your car."

"This time I might have to allow you." The accident had made her lose so much confidence. "I wouldn't like to do the slightest damage to your car."

"Not mine. A friend's."

"I see." She nibbled her lip. "If it wouldn't be too

much trouble. I have many talents but I'm not the greatest parker in the world."

"So you've said." He took her arm lightly though he might as well have shaken her such was her reaction. "Won't be more than five minutes, James."

"Take your time." James was doing his level best to assess this surprising situation, but was content to let fate take its course.

"Are you really meeting anybody?" Royce McQuillan asked when they were out on the street.

"I wonder you doubt me." If he hadn't released her she would have had to pull away.

"I do." He wondered what it would be like to kiss her mouth. *Hard.* Kiss the curve of her neck, the swell of her breast. Dangerous to have such thoughts about someone so young. Too young. He remembered James had told him all about his niece's twenty-first birthday party. But hang on, that had to be a year or more ago. Time went so swiftly.

"Stay like that," he ordered when they reached the footpath alongside the parked cars. "Just give me your keys."

"You *will* be careful." She couldn't understand why she was trying to provoke him. She closed her eyes as their fingers touched.

He didn't bother to answer. Instead he crammed himself into her tiny car, shot back the driver's seat as far as it would go, then in a matter of moments had the car waiting, ready for her to get into it and drive away.

"How very nice of you," she said, unable to get the cool satirical note out of her voice. She stood well back while he extricated himself from her car.

"A pleasure, Miss Russell. You quite interest me."

"Surely I'm not important enough for that?" She slipped into the driver's seat, aware she was being drawn into a dark whirlpool.

"I suspect not," he gave a low laugh, "nevertheless you might tell me why a beautiful girl like yourself, a gifted performer, would want to hide herself away in the wilds. You have an aura of intense excitement swirling all around you yet you want to get away. You must have some idea what station life would be like? You'd be so isolated much of the time."

"I know that." Her eyes looked straight ahead.

"So what's the reason?" His voice was like black velvet against her skin. "You've split with a boyfriend? You've changed your mind about your big career?"

Some things you couldn't help. "My career is *demolished*, Mr. McQuillan," she gritted, her voice harsh so she could keep it steady. "Thank you for helping me out. Of course if you hadn't parked so close behind me you wouldn't have had to worry."

The whole attitude of his lean powerful body changed. "Look," he said.

"No, *you* look." She lifted a hand in farewell and drove off.

She could still see him in her rear-view mirror. He was standing in the middle of the quiet street looking after her. God! He probably thought she was mad. She didn't have any appointment at the Conservatorium to keep. She couldn't bear to go home. Glenda's manner was so unpleasant these days. She'd thought to get rid of me but my accident changed that. It changed everything.

Tears sprang to Carrie's eyes but she blinked them away furiously. No use crying. What's done was done. Like Jamie said, she had to pick up the pieces and find strategies to propel her through life.

CHAPTER TWO

WHEN he returned to James' office, Royce got straight to the point. "Your niece just shocked me by telling me her career is demolished. What on earth happened? You've never said anything."

James found himself apologising. "Of course I should have. To be honest, Royce, I haven't felt able to talk about it. Carrie has grieved. We've all grieved for almost a year. She was involved in a car crash the very afternoon she had word she'd secured a place at the Julliard Academy in New York. The accident wasn't all that bad. A friend's car and a taxi collided. Carrie broke a couple of ribs, suffered a few abrasions but the worst part was the little finger of her right hand was very badly broken. The orthopaedic man did a marvellous job. For most purposes it's perfectly all right. She's still a highly accomplished pianist but he warned us the finger won't stand up to the rigours of a concert career. It will let her down, perhaps during a performance. I haven't got words for how we feel. Carrie has changed in little telling ways. But she's very brave. A fighter. In many ways she's been fighting all her life."

"You mean in terms of her relationship to her stepmother?" Royce asked perceptively.

James trusted this man so he gave an unhappy nod. "Like Carrie, my sister was so beautiful. Unforgettable really. When she died—a tragic accident, she fell and struck her head—Carrie was only three. Her father nearly went out of his mind. Jeff and I have never been close friends so I wasn't able to help him as I could have had things been different. He started to drink pretty heavily.

He hadn't before and he doesn't now, but out of his despair came a very quick second marriage. Glenda, his present wife, was his secretary. It appears she'd always been in love with him.''

"So she made things happen," Royce said quietly.

"Yes." James swallowed hard. "Melissa was born soon after. Carrie was never wanted by her stepmother. Her father adores her but he doesn't understand her any more than he understood my sister. Glenda is always very careful when Jeff's around but the relationship seen through my eyes and my wife's has never been caring. Not affectionate. Certainly not loving. To compound it all Carrie was by far the brighter child in the family. As you'll know from that photograph she was the prettiest little girl imaginable. She shone in the classroom. Right from the beginning she was brilliant at the piano, which I insisted she learn in remembrance of her mother who was a fine pianist, as was my mother. It runs in the family.''

"So the stepmother was not only jealous of her husband's attention to his firstborn she was jealous and resentful of her capabilities," Royce remarked.

"I'm afraid so. Carrie was always classed as a gifted child. Glenda saw the two girls in competition, which was sad for Melissa. Melissa had her mother's views and attitudes forced on her. I think the two girls could have been good friends but Glenda didn't want that. She wouldn't *permit* it."

"And Catrina's father didn't put a stop to this?" Royce asked almost curtly.

James shook his head. "Glenda is clever. Outwardly she's as proud of Carrie and her achievements as ever Jeff is. Inwardly I think she struggles with her rage. She was thrilled at the thought of Carrie's securing a place at the Julliard. That would have taken Carrie off her hands. Very very sadly it didn't happen."

"I'm sorry I didn't *know,*" Royce said, like he bitterly regretted the fact.

"I think I would have told you at some point but you've had lots of problems of your own, Royce," James answered in a conciliatory voice.

"Your niece is very unhappy."

It couldn't be denied. "She's struggling to overcome it. She hasn't touched the piano since the accident."

"So what is she doing with herself?" Royce McQuillan asked outright. "Teaching? That would be very hard at this point."

"*Very.* Her whole training has been geared to performance."

"I don't think she's governess material," Royce said. "Too many strong emotions working through her. A trauma to battle down. I was looking for a quiet capable young woman who wouldn't be discontented far away from boyfriends and the city life."

"I agree. I don't think Carrie is governess material, either, but she made it clear to me she wants to get right away from the world of music. For a time."

"*How* long?" Royce asked in his direct manner.

'Who would know?'' There was deep concern in James' voice. "I think Carrie feels all the pain and bitter disappointments like it was yesterday. She's right about one thing. She's great with children. Or she was until her world changed. She had such sparkle. Such vitality. Saddest to me is she's lost a lot of her natural confidence."

"Her accident has made her fearful?"

"Of certain things, yes," James agreed. "Her father would never hear of her leaving home. She's tried before but a large extent with her studies she's been dependent on him. He wouldn't thank me for interfering in any way. As I say, we don't get on. But Carrie told me today she is determined on moving out."

Royce didn't give that another moment's consideration. "It sounds like the obvious solution. Where will she go?" He narrowed his brilliant eyes.

"Wherever she wants to go. Liz and I will help her. Carrie is the love of our lives. She's given us such joy. She'll have a battle with her father, though. He's a born controller." James' largely hidden antipathy came through.

"Except he lost control all those years ago."

James nodded. "All that's history. Almost any other young woman would have made a better mother for Carrie than Glenda. A better mother for Melissa in a way although Glenda dotes on her. They present a united front socially but it's really a dysfunctional family."

"Then it can't be nice for Catrina to be around."

In that moment Royce McQuillan made the decision to act.

Carrie spent another hour in town drifting through a department store, buying nothing. Nothing appealed. She was simply putting off the moment she had to return home. There was such a soul-destroying drawing up of sides; Glenda and Melissa; she and her father. Instead of taking any advantage from the situation Carrie had found it a real burden knowing her father enjoyed her company better than her sister's. Not only that, he made no bones about showing it. His insensitivity had created many problems. She'd had the unenviable role of being the favourite. It had caused a lot of pain. On all sides.

Now that Carrie was a woman, Glenda hated her. Carrie felt almost positive Glenda felt no guilt because of it. Now that she wasn't going overseas to continue her studies Glenda was coming more and more into the open. When her father wasn't around Glenda didn't hesitate to use a cutting tongue. She did it with an air of triumph, knowing Carrie would never complain to her father. It had always been so. Carrie, even on Glenda's admission, had never used her unique position in her father's life to gain the ascendency or come between husband and wife. But it hadn't won her Glenda's friendship. That was the irony.

Driving into the garage, Carrie reflected the position and delightful appearance of their beautiful old colonial riverside home that proclaimed her father's affluence. The interior decoration was all Glenda. Glenda and the interior designer currently in favour. The spacious high-ceilinged rooms were choked with an overabundance of everything. Too much money gone mad, in Carrie's opinion. She always felt trapped inside.

The splendid Steinway her father had brought for her when she was eleven years old and already showing signs of promise had been banished from the living room to the soundproof studio Glenda had convinced her father ''darling little Carrie'' must have. Her father hadn't taken all that much persuasion for the good reason much as he loved her and was proud of her successes, he couldn't bear to hear her practising. Her father, she had long since accepted, would never make a music lover. She had given up wondering how her mother and father had come together in the first place. ''Sex appeal,'' James maintained. ''Jeff always was this great big handsome virile guy. They had little or nothing in common.''

Glenda and her father had a good deal in common; likes, dislikes, mutual interests. That didn't prevent her father revealing on rare occasions the unique place Caroline, his first wife, had had in his life. To this day Carrie thought he was tormented by it. The sudden violent loss. The end of a golden period in his life. A golden period that had never really started for her. She was deprived and she knew it. No one should have to do without a mother. Her immersion in her studies, her preoccupations with suc-

ceeding as a pianist, could have been the result of too little
bonding at home. Her music had shut her off from
Glenda's own unresolved resentments. She had poured out
her own yearnings on a keyboard. Now she had the feeling
of being profoundly at a disadvantage. At Glenda's mercy
unless she moved out. Ultimately though, it was her father
she would have to confront. This was the father who had
told her not so long ago if she left home it would break
his heart.

She let herself into the house quietly, coming in through
the rear door so she could escape to her bedroom. She
couldn't let these feelings of isolation get a hold on her.
It was a tragedy her stepmother and her own sister offered
her no support at this bad time, but she wasn't alone. She
had James and Liz, a whole lot of friends. The only thing
was most of her friends were fellow musicians. Their ca-
reers went on. Hers had badly faltered.

Someone was in her room. She knew it before she
opened the door. Melissa was standing in front of the mir-
rored wall of wardrobes, holding one of Carrie's evening
dresses to her body. The dress she had last performed in.
It had a shell top, a beautiful full skirt, and was a rich
orange, a difficult colour but it suited her.

"Hi, what are you doing?" Carrie tried not to show any
irritation. Melissa was always borrowing her things when
she had much more of her own. Items she wouldn't have
loaned under any circumstances. Melissa wasn't a lender.

"We didn't expect you home," Melissa said, continuing
to preen. "I'd like to wear this on Saturday. Can I?"

Carrie had to smile.

"Mel it won't fit you," she pointed out reasonably.
"The skirt will be too long, for one thing." Melissa was
petite if well covered. "It won't even suit you. We're different sizes, different styles. I love you in red. It brings

your colouring to life.'' She said it naturally, helpfully, but it angered Melissa.

''That's it! Go on, remind me. I *need* bringing to life.''

Carrie didn't worsen the situation by saying she did. ''We all benefit from wearing the colours that suit us. Don't get cranky for no reason,'' Carrie implored.

''Oh, and you aren't?'' Melissa turned around to throw the dress on the bed. ''The tragedy queen with the little smashed finger. Who said you were going to be a concert pianist anyway? If you'd ever got there you'd have probably found plenty better than you. You were just a big fish in a little bowl. New York is the centre of the world.''

''Well, I'm not going, Mel. So settle down. I'm not a whinger, either, so don't try pinning that on me.''

''Why, will you tell Dad?'' Melissa looked back belligerently, her voice on the rise, a pretty girl, dark curly hair, hazel eyes, a little overweight, but the expression on her face made Carrie want to give up.

''We can't talk, can we?'' she said quietly, feeling pretty well numb inside. ''We're sisters. That's wasting a valuable relationship.''

''Sisters?'' Melissa shouted, her face energised by jealousy. She followed Carrie up closely, hands on hips, obviously spoiling for a fight. ''Does that mean we're supposed to love one another?''

''It happens in most families.'' Carrie turned, picking up her dress and carrying it to the wardrobe.

''But you're too good for us, Carrie. Too clever for Mum and me. Mum says having you around has ruined our lives.''

Though the sort of stuff Glenda fed her daughter made Carrie feel sick to the stomach, she faced her sister calmly. ''How do you want me to react, Mel? Scream back? I was little more than a baby when my mother died. Three. I didn't want to come between anyone. I'd have adored having my own mother. You might think of that.''

"Oh, for God's sake, the gorgeous, the beautiful, the adorable Caroline.'' Melissa's pretty face was working.

"Who died when she was only a few years older than me,'' Carrie retaliated. "Thank *you*, Melissa. Doesn't that defuse your rage a little? She had her whole life in front of her.''

"But haven't you ever thought she's more glorious in death,'' Melissa cried almost hysterically. "That's what Mum says.''

"Then Mum has a lot to answer for.'' Carrie felt her own temper rise.

"You hate her, don't you? You hate me,'' Melissa insisted, dragging at her curls roughly.

"Mel, that's so unfair.'' Carrie put her hand on her stepsister's arm, grateful Melissa didn't shake it off. "That's some dreadful propaganda Glenda has fed you. It desperately hurt me to hear you say that. Glenda and I might never get on, but I wouldn't like to lose you. We're *blood*.'' She could feel Melissa trembling.

"How dare you!'' a voice shouted from the door. Glenda dressed to the nines was standing there quivering with outrage.

"For what it's worth,'' she fixed her greenish eyes on Carrie, "I'm your stepmother. I've looked after you and looked after you *well* for all these years, you ungrateful creature. Now you try to turn Melissa against me.''

"Oh, please, Mum, don't start,'' Melissa wailed, her eyes filling with tears.

"Look how you've upset her,'' Glenda accused.

Carrie took a deep breath. "Why don't you stop right now, Glenda,'' she said. "I'm having a bad enough time without your starting.''

"Is it pity you want?" Glenda demanded, her expression distorted.

'Understanding might say it,' Carrie answered briefly.

"You think yourself so extraordinary," Glenda said. "Anyone would think you were the only one who has ever suffered a setback. Between ourselves I've had a lot to contend with."

"You've never had talent like Carrie's," Melissa burst out unexpectedly. "I've never heard her big noting herself, either."

Glenda's impeccably made-up face drained of colour. She looked at her daughter as though she couldn't understand what she was saying. "Excuse me, Melissa, haven't I heard you endlessly complaining about Carrie's airs and graces?"

Melissa's reaction was even more unexpected. "Maybe I'm just jealous," she said. "I'd give anything to get covered in glory. To be lovely. Just a tiny bit like Carrie. To see Dad's eyes light up. To feel his pride in me. I'd have given anything to be Dad's perfect little girl. Ah, hell...." Melissa couldn't bear it any longer. She broke into sobs, trying to flee the room but Glenda stopped her forcibly, grabbing her wrists.

"My darling, don't you ever put yourself down. Your father *adores* you."

"Like hell he does, Mum. Beside Carrie I'm pathetic. A failure. I couldn't even get a place at uni. Dad was so disappointed in me."

"Ah, don't, Mel. Please don't." Carrie was deeply affected; answering tears sprang to her eyes. "What's so important about going to university? You'll find something you love doing."

"Then tell me what it is." Melissa was back to shouting. "I can't do a damn thing. I'm stupid. We all know that."

"You haven't begun to find yourself," Carrie said. "You have to try things, Mel. You're the best cook in the house."

"I beg your pardon." Glenda, who took particular pride in her culinary skills, looked affronted.

"Why not train to be a chef?" Carrie suggested. "You have a real way with food and food preparation. The way you're always experimenting and making new dishes."

"A chef!" Glenda looked totally taken aback though she couldn't deny Melissa was very good. "What nonsense you talk. Mel is able to turn out an excellent meal— perhaps a touch too exotic. I don't want her spending her time hanging around restaurants."

"She has to train first."

Melissa looked astonished. "Why not?"

"Oh, please!" Glenda shook all over in disgust. "Your father is a rich man, Melissa. Come to that, you don't have to work at all. You can help me."

"How? Chauffeur you around all day?" Melissa looked over at Carrie and actually smiled at her. "Do you think I could become a chef?"

"Of course I do," Carrie said briskly. "I'm greatly surprised you haven't thought of it before."

"Now look here, Carrie," Glenda began a shade helplessly. "Don't go putting foolish ideas into Melissa's head."

"It's quite an attractive idea," said Melissa, now oddly calm.

"My God!" Glenda held her head. "I want you out of here, Carrie," she said harshly. "I don't care how you do it—what you say to your father—I want you *out*. You've disrupted my home long enough."

Even Melissa flinched. "Mum don't!"

"That's all right." Carrie looked at Melissa reassuringly. "In lots of ways it will be better if I go."

"Not when you're being ordered out," Melissa said. "That's dreadful."

"Keep out of this, Melissa," her mother warned sharply, her expression furious. "Do you think because Carrie has suggested a job for you it's going to make things better? You girls have had a very spiky relationship for years. You want your father's attention? You'll get more of it with Carrie gone."

"Well, maybe..." Melissa looked confused.

"So that's settled," Carrie said, trying to absorb the blows. "I'll speak to Dad then I'll set about finding a place of my own."

"I'm sure you'll be a lot happier in it, Carrie," Glenda said in a much gentler tone, though the expression on her face was almost exultant. "You must realise how I've tried, I've..." She broke off, diverted by the sound of the front door chimes. "That must be the florist," she murmured, looking a whole lot brighter. "I've ordered a new arrangement for the entrance hall. Leave your sister now, Melissa, and come downstairs. I'm sure Carrie has lots to think about."

Carrie felt cut to the bone. Hot tears welled but she fought them back. She'd done enough crying in her pillow. It was time to rise above it. A few moments later Melissa rushed back into the room, appearing surprised, but very pleasantly so. "Carrie, there's someone downstairs who wants to see you. The best-looking guy I've ever seen in my life. You've gotta come clean."

"About what, then? Who is it?" Carrie turned away; quickly brushing a few unshed tears off her eyelashes.

"Says his name is Royce McQuillan. Got a great voice. Real cool."

"You're joking?" But Carrie knew that she wasn't.

"Mum offered him something but he didn't want it.

They're in the living room talking. Mum seems to be enjoying it. She loves the tall dark handsome types."

"I'll be there in a moment," Carrie said, walking through to the adjoining bathroom to run a comb through her hair, but mostly to check the sign of tears didn't show.

They did. Or she thought they did, she was so emotional.

"You don't have to touch anything," Melissa said, following her into the en suite. "You're perfect. You've got this incredible skin. Why haven't I? You never have a breakout. It's not fair."

"We both know you have very good skin, too, Mel. And big hazel eyes. I don't have a curl in sight."

"Curls aren't special," said Melissa.

Glenda and Royce McQuillan were seated in the living room, apparently enjoying a pleasant conversation. "Oh, there you are, dear." Effortlessly Glenda assumed a fond voice. But then she'd had so much practice. "You have a visitor."

Royce McQuillan stood up, unbearably handsome and *physical*. Giving her that coolly sexy smile. "Catrina, it's wonderful to see you. I just happened to be in the area."

"How nice of you to call in." She marvelled her own voice rippled with pleasure.

"I'll be flying home tomorrow," he explained, "I thought we might have dinner tonight if you're free?"

"That would be lovely." Such an unexpected saviour!

He had moved right up to her, taking her hand, staring down into her face. "So I'll see you tonight then?"

"Marvellous. I'm looking forward to it. What time?" She almost begged him to take her with him.

He shot a cuff, and glanced at his watch. "If you could be ready at seven? I haven't given you much warning."

"Seven will be fine," she said, with a quick smile. "I won't be late."

"I'll pick you up." He turned to look at Glenda who was staring at them both in a kind of open-mouthed fascination. "A pleasure meeting you, Mrs. Russell. You, too, Melissa." He gave her a smile that might haunt her for the rest of her days. "Catrina has spoken of you both. I must apologise for tearing off but I'm cutting it rather fine as it is. I have to see someone before I go back to the hotel."

Glenda rose, looking at Carrie as though she was precious. "It's a great pity you'll miss my husband," she said. "He's working late tonight. You know how it is?"

"My busiest times are the mornings. I'm a cattle man, Mrs. Russell. My home is North Queensland."

"How exciting!" Glenda was studying him in detail, wondering where on earth Carrie had found this prize.

"It's a very beautiful part of the world, north of Capricorn," McQuillan said, towering over the petite, very trim Glenda. "Catrina, would you like to walk me to my car?" he asked with a turn of his head.

She smiled at him and he smiled back.

"Goodbye, then." He gave the mesmerised women, Glenda and Melissa, a charming salute. "I'm sure we'll meet again."

"That's great!" The nineteen-year-old Melissa burst out.

They walked in silence out of the house and along the front path bordered by an avenue of palms and farther back an avalanche of azaleas and flowering shrubs intoxicating in their perfume.

"You've been crying?" he said.

"I have not." She knew she sounded nervy.

"Your stepsister doesn't look in the least like you."

"Not surprising, I'm said to be the image of my mother."

"She must have been very lovely."

"Yes." Carrie answered simply as though it wasn't a compliment to herself.

"I can well see your stepmother might give you a hard time," he remarked rather grimly.

She turned her head in surprise. Glenda had been at her social best. "Didn't she act welcoming enough?"

"Indeed she did. She was very pleasant. I just happened to spot something in her eyes. Are you all right?" he asked after a minute.

"I'm absolutely fine." Carrie decided it was time to get right to the point. "Why are you here, Mr. McQuillan? Somehow you've given my stepmother and sister the impression we're…friends."

Quirky little brackets appeared at the side of his mouth. "Well, it's hard *not* to like you, Catrina. And I have to say it was good to find out you're not nervous of me *personally*."

"Jamie told you about my accident," she said a little fiercely.

"He did." He opened the front gate for her, marking the beauty of her hair in the golden sunlight. "I wish he had told me before. We've become closer than the usual solicitor/client relationship, but he loves you so much he found your pain unbearable. I can understand that."

"Can you?"

His smile twisted. "You don't think I've ever loved anyone?"

She stared up at him, the brilliance of the sun flecking her eyes with gold sparks. "I'm sorry. What you must think of me! Of course you have. You *do*."

"That's better, Catrina," he said crisply. "If I were a betting man as well as a horse breeder I wouldn't put money on whether you and I will get on."

"I share your alarm," she said, too agitated to watch her tongue.

"Very wise of you," he drawled, holding her gaze for a minute. "It seems to me, however, having heard your story, I can help you out of a very difficult situation. At least for a time. You on the other hand might well be able to help me with Regina."

Carrie drew in a raw ragged breath. "You mean you're *hiring* me?"

"What does that bloody woman say to you?" he asked, his scrutiny intense.

For a moment she felt drained of all strength. "I'm not her child, *her* daughter. I desperately need to get away."

"So she won't damage you further."

"You can't *know*," she protested. "Glenda isn't all that bad."

"Isn't she? James filled me in. Besides, I've had a pretty event-packed life. I know a lot more than you, Miss Twenty-Two."

"A great deal more," Carrie said. "I'm sorry I'm being rude. You must bring out that side of me."

"I expect being mad at the world has helped a lot." He studied her with a mixture of mockery and sympathy.

"It's not easy to come to terms with the shattering of one's dreams."

"My feelings exactly," he replied with quiet irony. "You can tell me all about it over dinner." He bent suddenly and, while she felt a rush of pure panic, kissed her cheek.

"What did you do that for?" She tried but couldn't find more than a shadow of her voice.

"What do you think, Catrina? For the benefit of step-mamma. She hasn't moved away from the curtains."

"She'll tell Dad!"

"I don't care who she tells. Do you? Besides a peck on

the cheek doesn't mean I'm about to steal Jeff Russell's little girl.''

"Then *who* exactly are you supposed to be?" she asked with difficulty.

He gave a brief amused laugh. "I know it's a dreadful role but at the moment I'm your knight in shining armour. Don't worry, Catrina. We'll decide on a story tonight. Now I simply must go." Briskly he moved around to the driver's seat of the parked Jaguar. "By the way…" A moment's hesitation before he got behind the wheel. "Do you have a yellow dress in your wardrobe?"

She was astonished by the turns in the conversation. Astonished at his being there at all. "You like yellow?"

"I think it would be perfect for you, Catrina," he said as though he knew she needed cheering up. "I want you to dress up. We'll go to Vivaldi's. I'm in the mood for something grand."

It was the perfect way for a knight to exit, Carrie thought.

When she returned to the house, Glenda and Melissa were very nearly dancing on the marble floor of the entrance hall in their excitement and need to know.

"What have you got to say for yourself?" Glenda challenged her. "You *are* a dark horse." She laughed with a shadow of bitter envy. "So secretive. Were you frightened your father was going to forbid you to see him? Is he married? He *must* be married. There isn't a woman alive who'd make the mistake of letting him get away."

"Come on, Carrie," Melissa urged when her stepsister remained silent. "At least you can tell us now?"

When she was on the verge of being thrown out. "Why exactly, Melissa?" Carrie asked. "It's not your business really. Now more than ever. Wasn't it decided I move out only minutes before…Royce arrived?'' She barely tripped over his Christian name.

"Is it possible you're thinking of moving in with him?'' Glenda abruptly questioned, her eyes narrowing to mere slits.

"Why would that upset you, Glenda?'' Carrie said it as though it were of no consequence.

"You know I have to tell your father.''

Angered but trying to hold on to herself, Carrie made a move toward the stairs. "Glenda you have no authority over me,'' she said quietly. "I'm twenty-two years of age. I love my father but it's high time I stood on my own two feet. Royce McQuillan is a friend. He comes from a highly respected family with a fine pioneering name. He *was* married, as it happens. He has one child, a little girl in his custody.''

"You mean he's divorced?'' Glenda gasped, her skin flushing a dark red.

Carrie hesitated, one hand on the banister. "Unhappily many marriages lead to divorce, Glenda. The happily ever after we'll have to leave to you and Dad.''

"Are you in love with him, Carrie?'' Melissa called, her hazel eyes round with excitement. "You must be. He's gorgeous.''

"No, I'm not in love with him, Mel.'' Carrie paused on the first landing, wondering what they would say if they knew she and Royce McQuillan had only just met.

"Don't think you can escape your father's questioning,'' Glenda cried in a threatening tone. "He looked a dangerous man to me. Striking, rich, years older than you. Light-years in experience, all that suave charm. Without doubt you're having an affair. A secret affair it now seems.''

"The one thing you won't be able to interfere in, Glenda,'' Carrie called down lightly.

"Your father will be shocked when he discovers it." Glenda moved to the base of the staircase, looking up.

"Well, maybe he will be, but Dad trusts me to look after myself, to do the right thing."

"And to think the way you've taken us in!" Glenda was the very picture of betrayal. "Pretending your life was ruined and all the time you had a man like Royce McQuillan tucked away. McQuillan....McQuillan...surely I know the name?" Glenda shook her head vigorously as if to clear it. "It will come to me," she muttered.

"Gosh, I think it's wonderful!" Melissa exclaimed, totally ignoring her mother and her sentiments. "You lucky thing, Carrie, you've found your dream man."

At least one who might take me out of my misery.

She had the choice of two dresses, both slip dresses, very much in fashion. One white chiffon with yellow stripes and yellow daisy appliqué. The other, which she finally settled on, golden-yellow chiffon with a rather exquisite floral print; gold high-heeled evening sandals on her feet. Her father's twenty-first birthday present, which had been made to order, went perfectly with it. A large topaz pendant set in 18 kt gold hung from a beautiful gold chain with topaz gold earrings to match.

She was applying a dab of perfume to the insides of her wrists when Melissa came through the bedroom door without knocking, a large book under her arm.

"Mum finally cracked it," she chortled, opening up the coffee-table-sized book at a marked page. "'Kings of the Cattle Country,'" she read. "Your boyfriend's grandad is in it. The book's a bit old but it's all about the cattle empires and today's cattle kings. Here he is, Sir Andrew McQuillan, the master of Maramba Downs. A pretty glamorous figure, don't you think? You can easily see the resemblance. There's a picture of the homestead, too. It looks out on a lagoon. It looks fabulous. *Huge!* And there's a photo of a lot of cattle standing in a kind of billabong with the Great Dividing Range or spurs of it in the background. Tropical North Queensland. Don't you want to look?''

Carrie pretended to be unimpressed. ''I know all about it,'' she said casually. Lord forgive me for the white lie. Nevertheless she couldn't resist moving behind the shorter Melissa to glance over her shoulder, catching an aerial view of the station and its numerous outbuildings and a large herd of Brahmins penned in a holding yard.

''I'm just staggered you never told us, Carrie,'' Melissa said, her voice light with disbelief.

''There's nothing to tell,'' Carrie answered mildly. ''I don't even know Royce particularly well.''

''He *kissed* you,'' Melissa pointed out, making it sound like a passionate embrace.

''On the cheek. A friendly farewell.''

Melissa, looking unconvinced, returned to the book. '''The McQuillan operation encompasses a chain of strategically placed stations to safeguard against drought stretching from the Channel Country in the far southwest right to the Northern Territory border,''' she read. ''Here, I can't hold this, it's too heavy.'' She set the book down hard on the long chest at the foot of Carrie's bed. ''You look beautiful,'' she suddenly said at a rush, a trace of real caring in her eyes. ''I bet *he* thinks so, too.''

''Thanks, Mel.'' Carrie gave her stepsister a poignant little smile, wondering how Glenda could have spread such devastation. ''I want to say I'm sorry you think I robbed you of Dad's attention. I never wanted that.''

There was a long wait for a response. ''On my good days I realise that,'' Mel said with a kind of embarrassment. ''The trouble is, *always was,* you're far more *everything* than I am. It's not easy being outshone. I guess that's why Mum and I are always attacking you. I'm sorry for that, Carrie. If you'd have been ordinary like me we'd have gotten along fine.''

"But aren't you going to be a cordon bleu?" Carrie asked in a challenging voice, catching up her gold evening purse. "What's ordinary about that?"

"I hope Dad lets me."

This could be their last conversation for a while, Carrie thought. "My advice, Mel," she said earnestly, "is don't let him stop you. You've got to make a life for *yourself*."

"Well, we'll see." Melissa blushed. "Enjoy yourself, Carrie. Deep down I think I really love you."

CHAPTER THREE

ROYCE MCQUILLAN arrived on the dot of seven, spiriting her away with such practiced charm Glenda was left with very little to say.

"I don't think I could have liked a dress more if I'd picked it out myself," he complimented Catrina as they walked to the car. "No trace of tears, either," he added, experiencing a powerful urge to see this young woman out of the house. The "atmosphere" could have been cut with a knife.

"You're just too observant," Carrie managed wryly, so overwhelmed by his sudden appearance in her life she was floating.

"Very much so," he said briefly, not adding because it would panic her she had aroused in him a potentially dangerous sexual response. He couldn't dress it up as anything else. Now he had more or less committed himself to taking her under his roof. This beautiful young woman wasn't in the least what he wanted as a governess for Regina. She had problems of her own to cope with, most notably coming to terms with the destruction of a promising career. That presented quite a trauma in itself. He had to be mad. Yet her light fragrance filled the interior of the car with such images of spring blossom and sweet breezes. "Your stepmother seems most insistent I meet your father," he remarked when they were underway, driving down the street with its splendid old colonial homes set in leafy gardens and river frontages.

Carrie glanced out the window, into the star-filled indigo night. "Please don't be angry, or worse, *laugh*, but she's under the impression you and I are having a secret affair. Nothing I could possibly say would affect her thinking. Glenda believes what she wants to believe.''

''That was fairly obvious. So what did you tell her?''

''Only that you were a friend. That you were divorced and you have a little girl aged six.''

''Nothing about coming back with me to Maramba?''

She was shocked by the effect of his words on her. ''I wasn't totally sure you wanted me,'' she confessed.

''I would have hoped for someone quite different.''

She turned her amber head, the long full pageboy swinging to her bare shoulders. ''What have you got against me? My education hasn't been neglected. I was an excellent student. Teaching a six-year-old her lessons couldn't be difficult.''

He glanced at her. ''Catrina, I'm not referring to that aspect of it. I'm not telling you anything you don't already know. You're *over* qualified and you're lovely, not the sort of young woman who can escape into the background.''

''Of course I am,'' Catrina contradicted, a soft flush rising to her face. ''I've had to be very self-effacing at home. My stepmother and I have had a *very* difficult relationship. It's useless to hide the fact her attitude poisoned my relationship with my sister. She set us up as competitors and it wasn't fair to either of us. If you want me to disappear into the furniture I'll do it.''

''Okay.'' He laughed. ''You really *want* this job?''

''At the moment I desperately need it,'' she admitted frankly. ''Before you arrived this afternoon, Glenda and I had a few words. She wants me out.''

''Does she!'' His voice deepened with evident disapproval. ''What does your sister have to say about that?''

''Mel does what she's told. She's only nineteen. She doesn't have a job yet.''

''I understood from James you're very much the apple

of your father's eye.'' He eased into the freeway traffic, a
scintillating ribbon of light.

"I suppose you could say that's been a lot of the trouble.
I don't make mischief. Dad misses a lot that goes on. He's
a very busy man and Glenda is always very careful when
he's around.''

"How will he take your coming with me?'' he asked
bluntly, turning to look at her as they stopped at the red
light.

"Badly, I would think.''

"You're twenty-two. You can't be Daddy's little girl
forever. I'll speak to him, naturally.''

"You will?''

"Of course.'' His mouth compressed at her surprised
tone. "I wouldn't want *my* daughter haring off to the wilds
with a complete stranger. Moreover a divorced man. It
might help for you to know—you're so traumatised you
haven't asked—I have a fairly full household so you'll be
well chaperoned. There's my grandmother, Louise. My father's mother. She's into her eighties now and a remarkable woman. Then there's my uncle Cam, my father's
younger brother, and his second wife, Lindsey. His first
wife was killed in a riding accident on the station. A great
tragedy. I was only a boy when it happened but I clearly
remember how warm and attractive she was. She and my
mother were very close. In fact she was my mother's
bridesmaid. Cam remarried only two years ago. A whirl-
wind affair. Lyn swept him off his feet. And of course
there's Regina.''

"Your uncle's wife can't help with her lessons?'' Carrie
asked.

"Children aren't Lyn's scene,'' he answered briefly.

"Oh! How depressing for Regina.''

"We've had two governesses already.''

"I hope they were suitably plain?" she couldn't resist asking, but absolutely sweetly.

"To tell you the truth I didn't notice. One was better than the other but unfortunately neither could handle the job. Regina didn't make things easy. She can be a little terror."

"I'd like to meet her." Carrie laughed.

"You should do that more often," he commented.

"What?" He had *such* an expressive voice; her musical ear was vastly unsettled by it.

"Laugh."

"Does Regina see her mother?" she asked.

"She hasn't seen her for some considerable time. It's very hard on Regina, but it suits me. My ex-wife is not my favourite person."

"You must have loved her once?" she commented in a low voice.

"I thought I did." There was an underlying note of self-derision.

"I'm sorry."

"Nothing for you to worry about." He turned his handsome head briefly. "My wife's sister, Ina, comes to visit from time to time."

"Regina would enjoy that." Catrina absorbed this new piece of information with a sense of affirmation in family, but she was soon put straight.

"Not noticeable," Royce McQuillan commented dryly, "although Ina is very much like Sharon. I suppose as a family we're every bit as dysfunctional as yours appears to be."

The maître d' showed them to a candle-lit table for two with the best view of the multicoloured dappled river and the city night-time glitter from high-rise towers to spanning bridges. What was total astonishment at what was happening to her if not a cure for the miseries? Carrie thought. She felt stirred and excited; her confidence such, she resisted the temptation to smooth her shoulder-length hair, which in fact looked perfect. Before today she had never even heard of Royce McQuillan, tonight she was dining out with him, attracting a great deal of attention in the process. Without vanity Carrie didn't fully understand the attention from the spacious beautifully appointed dining room was about equally divided. The men, recognising a beautiful young woman when they saw one, were looking at her; the women couldn't force their eyes away from the charismatic Royce McQuillan. Carrie in fact had to swallow every time she looked at him. He was an extraordinarily compelling man. A man who did things with style. Too daunting and too coolly charming all at the same time. Puzzlingly she vaguely resented it even as she blessed his intervention in her life. With Glenda on the attack she had been feeling all but worn out.

"Hungry?" he asked as Carrie began to peruse the lengthy menu.

"I can't honestly say I am." She was absorbing so much excitement from him it was frightening. "The turn of events left me unsettled. I never dreamed this morning I'd be having dinner like this tonight."

"I'm that kind of man," he answered casually. "You ought to try and relax. Have you been here before?"

"No." She shook her head, glancing around the room. It was decorated in luxurious European style in keeping with its name. Beautiful blue moiré silk on the walls, large floral paintings in gilded frames, dazzling chandeliers, impressive china, silver service, crystal, formally dressed guests. "My father and Glenda come here often. It's very impressive."

"So is the food." He scanned his own menu, his striking dark face downbent so she could study him without his noticing. The golden flame from the candle-flower arrangement centre table lent his skin the sheen of polished bronze. Hair and brows, ebony. "What about seafood? That's light."

It really didn't matter. She felt so strange she was content to follow his lead. The wine waiter approached and without even looking at the wine list or consulting Carrie—perhaps he knew full well how she was feeling— he ordered a vintage Bollinger.

"I don't believe anyone can have a glass of really good champagne without feeling better," he commented lightly. "Don't worry, Catrina, I'm not going to ply you with alcohol. I'm in pursuit of a governess, remember?"

"I know that," she responded a shade tartly.

"So why the look in those amber eyes?"

"Describe it," she challenged.

"All right." His tone was soothing. "You look like you're trying to decide whether you should pick up that daffodil skirt and run."

"Do you blame me?" she asked in a low voice. "You're a *stranger*."

"No I'm not." He looked at her amusedly. "I told you I'm your knight in shining armour."

"Dragooned into the job."

"Don't think that." His fingers just brushed the tip of hers yet she felt the hot wave of reaction wash over her from head to toe.

"That blush is exquisite, Catrina." He watched the apricot colour spread over her flawlessly creamy skin. "I haven't seen a woman blush for years. Make that a decade," he added rather bitterly.

Why wouldn't she blush with so much heat in her blood? "Perhaps we'd better establish at once exactly who I am," she suggested. On the defensive. "The new governess. An employee."

"Perhaps a distant cousin?" He held her golden gaze. "If you're uncomfortable with kissin' cousin."

She couldn't speak for a moment thinking this man unanswerable. "I can understand why the other governesses left and I don't believe Regina was all to blame," she finally managed briskly.

He smiled and the faintly saturnine expression was totally banished. Instead sensuality dwelt in the depths of his eyes. "If you think I teased *them* you couldn't be more mistaken. You're as unusual to me as I am to you. Besides with that little air of hauteur, you're exactly right to tease."

She knew she was playing with fire but the flame was too bright. "Perhaps now and again I might even respond?" she quietly replied, aware she was feeling a little dizzy and she hadn't even touched a single drop of wine.

For answer he turned his attention back to the leatherbound menu. "I'd like that, Catrina, but it won't actually happen. I think we both know where that path might lead."

She had never met nor expected to meet a man so dangerous, so mesmerizing in her life. For the first time since her accident she felt acutely alive, all her senses returned to her. Probably by tomorrow she'd return to earth with another sickening crash.

The food was superlative, the sauces that accompanied the seafood dishes so delicious, so creamy, so beautifully flavoured, she found she was hungry. Both had settled for a starter of Moreton Bay oysters in an amber-tinted champagne sauce with caramelised spring oysters followed by the lobster dish Vivaldi's was famous for, the main course. All through Royce McQuillan quietly entertained her with a fund of stories about station life, some of them brilliantly funny, deliberately so because he told her he liked to hear her laugh. It was when they were debating a dessert versus a cheese platter with the cheese platter ahead, that the strange harmony of the evening was shattered. With her back to the entry Carrie wasn't able to observe the late arrival of a very glamorous-looking foursome but she couldn't help remarking the spectacular change to Royce McQuillan's expression. Perceptibly the lean powerful body tautened, the brilliant black eyes became hooded and the muscles along his hard firm jaw line clenched.

She remained perfectly still, asking quietly. "Is everything all right?" Obviously it wasn't.

He frowned heavily. "A shame to have the evening ruined. Don't turn your head, it's possible they'll miss us."

Whoever they were. Faint hope, she thought, of missing him. Not with his height, breadth of shoulder and striking good looks.

In another few moments a woman's bright brittle voice exclaimed from somewhere just behind Carrie's shoulder. "But how absolutely charming!" The remark to Carrie's sensitive ear was charged with venom. Yet she fully expected Royce McQuillan to rise to his feet. Instead he remained seated, staring up at the ultra-slim woman who moved into view, standing over the table. How utterly sophisticated she looked! She wore a very sexy side-slit silver dress, her dark head with its full fringe pulled into a high knot with a long fall at the back. She was looking at Carrie oddly, pale blue eyes like ice chips. "Why, isn't she like a flower?" she cooed in a frankly sarcastic tone. "A bright orange lily. And so *young!* Aren't you going to introduce us, darling?"

"Sorry, Sharon," he drawled. "I'm not going to introduce you at all." The perturbation was now very successfully hidden beneath coolly amused detachment.

"A man like you always needs a beautiful woman around," the woman Sharon observed, continuing to stand there staring from Royce to Carrie with extraordinary intensity. "How are *you,* Babs?" she suddenly addressed

Carrie directly. "I'm Sharon McQuillan by the way. Yes, I *do* exist. Very much so. And you are?"

"No one of any interest, Mrs. McQuillan," Carrie replied, keeping her tone courteous but neutral.

"But I feel—I just *know*—you are." Clearly under the icy sarcasm Sharon McQuillan was disturbed, maybe even furious.

"You should just accept you're past tense, Sharon," Royce advised.

"I won't!" she responded, her expression so tight for a moment she looked almost plain. "You always were a cruel devil, Royce."

"I don't think that would stand up to examination." His answering tone though low definitely grated. "Anyway, don't let it bother you. I'm out of your life. Now why don't you rejoin your friends? They're throwing all sorts of looks in this direction. I see Ina is with you?"

Sharon McQuillan gave an odd almost contemptuous laugh. "Ina is very insecure. My sister has accepted she can't move out of my shadow. I'd appreciate it, too, Royce, if you didn't allow her to visit the station so frequently. Of course she's using poor Regina as an excuse. It's *you* she comes to see."

So that's it, Carrie thought, hearing the ring of truth.

"Still jealous of one another? I don't know how you find the energy." Royce McQuillan sounded sharply amused. "Why don't you leave quietly, Sharon? You've stood there long enough. It's rather sad."

Sharon McQuillan countered by leaning closer, her confident voice floundering slightly. "Don't let him humiliate you as he has humiliated me," she warned Carrie. "He might bewitch you now—he's bewitched us all—but he'll starve you of affection in the end. I know."

Empathy for another woman moved Carrie to respond. Rightly or wrongly, Sharon McQuillan was suffering.

"Mrs. McQuillan, I told you, you're making something out of nothing." Not that it was any of her business.

But Sharon McQuillan continued to stare bitterly into Carrie's great golden eyes. "I'm sorry, that's impossible to believe. I've had a lot of experience in these matters. You're *someone* in my husband's life."

Utterly fed up, Royce McQuillan rose to his impressive height, dominating both women. "Ex-husband, Sharon," he corrected her. "Surely it's not necessary to remind you? We'll say goodnight. Best wishes elude me."

It was then Sharon McQuillan made her move. She put one hand on his shoulder, then raised herself on tiptoes just long enough to land a kiss clearly meant for his mouth on his cheek. "'Night, darling," she breathed in a voice that combined ecstasy and torture. Then she rounded on Carrie, putting an oddly sympathetic expression on her face.

"Goodnight, Miss Who-ever-you-are. May I compliment you on your hair? It's absolutely beautiful. Though I can't distinguish if it's natural or from a bottle."

"You really need to look at the roots for help." Royce's voice had a hard mocking edge. "'Bye, Sharon. I won't forget to give your love to your daughter."

"Do that, darling." Sharon waved over her shoulder, already beginning to thread her way back to her table.

"Lord!" Carrie murmured after a long moment's hesitation. She was used to infighting but was unnerved by the quality of this exchange.

"'I'm sorry about that," Royce apologised. "The timing was terrible. It's the first time I've been out to dinner in months and I have to run into my ex-wife."

"It must have been very painful." She recognised his upset.

"Not in the way *you* mean. The pain is for Regina. Sharon rejected her from day one."

Carrie's own sense of fairness made her read for an excuse. "Could it have been possible she was suffering from postnatal depression?" she suggested.

He thought on that very briefly. "I do have sensitivity, Catrina," he answered, his handsome face dark and moody. "Sharon couldn't bond with her child because she *didn't want her.* She demonstrated that over and over again. Regina has never known a mother's love."

Carrie shook her head in a kind of denial. "That is so sad, but she must be very close to you?"

"Intensely so," he said in a gentler tone, "but unfortunately it involves a lot of screaming and yelling. Regina wants to come with me to places I can't possibly take her. She's only a little girl and I have a huge cattle chain to run. I have to be away from home at different times. I can't dance attendance on her and she can't and won't understand. In that way she's a little bit like her mother. In other ways, too. Sharon was always what they used to call 'highly strung.' I thought it was simply being spoiled rotten, but I soon learned."

"It's upset your evening."

"And yours." His voice was quiet. "You've gone pale."

"She still loves you," Carrie said.

He looked back into her eyes with brilliant irony. "Sharon can't bear to let go of anything she thinks is *hers.* Love doesn't come into it. She needs to retain possession."

Carrie wasn't convinced. "And her sister, Regina's aunt is with her? I don't want to turn my head but I can feel eyes boring into my back."

"All four pairs of them," he said. "The men because you're beautiful. Sharon and Ina have been in competition ever since I can remember and I've known them both forever. By and large Sharon always comes out the winner.

Why don't we have coffee somewhere else?" he suggested.

Carrie felt quite in control. "Please don't bother about me. I've had a very enjoyable time. I'm quite happy to go home."

"Surely that's just an expression." He raised a black brow.

"Yes it is," she was forced to admit. "I mean, I'm ready to go home."

He raised a hand to summon a waiter. "No, we'll have coffee," he said. "No need to rush. You know all the in places better than I do."

"Well, I know where they serve the best coffee," she said. "Look, I really don't…"

"Forget it," he said. It was as they were preparing to leave the restaurant that Sharon's younger sister, Ina, made her own move. She rushed up to them, a little breathless though Royce had acknowledged her presence with a little wave directed to her table.

"Royce!" she cried, smiling at him brilliantly. "How marvellous to see you. What brings you to town?"

"Business, of course." He accepted her quick peck on the cheek fairly charmingly. "How are you, Ina?" Again defying conventional manners he didn't introduce Carrie who took her cue and wandered a little way off.

The two sisters shared a strong resemblance, Carrie thought. Both tall, ultra-slim, dark-haired, light eyes, very sophisticated in their dress. The elder Sharon was the more striking, sexier, sharper, with a slightly febrile look about her. Ina appeared softer, less overwhelmingly self-confident. Her voice was more attractive, too, lacking her sister's less pleasant brittle note. Though she wasn't looking in their direction, Carrie was aware part of Ina's forward rush was to find out exactly who Carrie was. It could even have been at Sharon McQuillan's insistence. From all accounts, she was the dominant sister.

Carrie was pretending to be engrossed in a very beautiful arrangement of spring flowers when Royce returned to take her by the elbow. "I'm terribly, *terribly* sorry about that," he said. "You'll have to forgive my bad manners not introducing you but I don't want you drawn into this." He didn't add, though Carrie guessed, his ex-wife wouldn't rest until she had found out exactly who Carrie was. A private investigator wasn't out of the question. Sharon McQuillan had used one before.

"I didn't know I was so interesting," Carrie responded lightly, though she was becoming unbearably aware of his proximity.

"Extraordinarily enough, interest becomes fixated on anyone on my arm," he told her dryly.

They walked in what seemed a loaded silence along the brightly lit waterfront promenade with its strolling couples, the breeze fresh and clean, tangy with salt, the sky full of stars, the Milky Way a flittering trail of diamond daisies. Luxurious yachts were moored out front, the City Kats, the ferries in operation, the big beautiful paddlewheeler, *The Kookaburra Queen,* the cruise craft docked at the pier. Nearing where the Jag was parked on the street, a short distance from the restaurant, a very expensive sports car going much too fast suddenly shot out of a hotel drive causing Carrie to react with alarm. Her fears and anxieties had not diminished in the many long months since her accident. They had increased.

"Catrina, it's all right." Instantly his arm went around her, gathering her in. Just like that. Her body had come to rest against his, her head pressed into his shoulder. "There's always some fool showing off to his girlfriend," he muttered, staring after the car with its young male and female occupants. "Probably over the limit."

Carrie scarcely heard. Her whole body had dissolved. Or that was the way he made her feel? Liquified. She'd been much too busy with all her studies for a close relationship but she knew enough to realise real passion, *burning* passion, violent desire was unknown to her.

Until now.

How utterly senseless.

One of his arms was cradling her back. She only had to lift her head for her mouth to brush hotly against his brown throat. She knew she was trembling. Her body was emitting all the wrong signals; the most terrible folly of female surrender. She could inhale the wonderful male scent of him, the power and glamour, feel his masked strength. She even thought she murmured something. Or was it a soft moan that escaped her lips? This was a man who could break her heart. Instinct born of a lifetime of pain.

If Carrie was buckling under the weight of desire, Royce McQuillan, too, felt its extraordinary impact. How could feeling like this spring from nowhere? Her body was so soft, so female-fragile in his arms. He wanted to slip his other hand across her breast. He wanted to bring his mouth down on that alluring little beauty spot. He wanted to kiss her open mouth. He didn't want to stop there. He hadn't been celibate since he and Sharon had broken up. But he'd always known how to contain himself.

Until now.

His sudden violent need of her was akin to man's need of pure water. He had a clear image of himself in the desert. A dry canyon of reflected colours, his throat badly parched until he turned and saw a crystal spring. He wanted to gather the silvery droplets on his tongue...

How could one moment go on forever? He forced himself to breath deeply; telling himself it was a man's primitive response to a beautiful woman. But control didn't come easily when adrenaline was like fire in his blood.

She was resting her soft weight against him, her own breathing ragged.

God, what was happening, he thought, stultified at the speed of it? It was like being on a wild ride. Terrifying and at the same time exhilarating. He couldn't seem to contain the ferocity of desire despite the tight rein, as his fingers found her nape beneath the thick silk of her hair, traced the curve from neck to shoulder.

Stop now. He gave himself the stern warning though little frissons of arousal were running up his arm. Desire was hell. It ruined lives. Alive with self-contempt, he took her lovely face in one hand—he could feel the heat of her flush—his voice deeper than usual but fake-casual.

"I'd love to prolong the moment, Catrina," he said, "but there's someone on a bicycle about to ride over us." In fact the bike rider was walking his bike to the traffic lights. But no matter. He had to abide by the rules. This was one girl he couldn't ravish. God, he hardly knew her. Regina's new governess. A young woman with her own problems so the potential for trouble was enormous. He had to focus very hard on that.

CHAPTER FOUR

CARRIE had a task in front of her convincing her father she needed to get away. They were seated at the breakfast table—her father had delayed his leaving time for the office—and the atmosphere was very tense.

"But a governess, Carrie?" Jeff Russell exclaimed, hurt and surprise on his face. "Why on earth would you want to do something like that?" He made the job sound like the most menial of domestic positions. "You've spent all these years training to be a musician now you want to bury yourself in the jungles of North Queensland. I don't understand it. There must be something more to it. This man McQuillan," he asked forcefully, "have you fallen in love with him?"

Carrie stared back at her father without answering. She hadn't. She believed she hadn't. She didn't want to think it had happened. She had decided absolutely not to. Yet last night she could have stayed with him forever. At one point he could have picked her up and carried her right away. A fatal attraction? That's what it was. God, why not? The man was devastating.

"Carrie? Are you going to stay like that, not opening your mouth?" Jeff Russell, a dominating sort of man, demanded.

Carrie paid attention, her body taut and strained. "I'm sorry, Dad. I know you love me. I know you want the best for me, but I don't think you truly understand what my injury has done to me. I might sound spineless but it's upset my whole world. I just want to get away for a time. I don't want to have anything to do with the music scene."

Her father muffled an explosion of disbelief. "After all the money that's been spent on you. Why the price of the Steinway alone! Good God, what father pays that kind of money?" Jeff Russell threw up his hands in despair. "I don't know how you can think I don't care. You're *my daughter*." His dark blue eyes flashed. "I've always done my best for you. I can't let this happen."

Carrie clasped her two hands together to stop them trembling. Her father was such an overpowering man. "I'm twenty-two, Dad," she pointed out quietly. "An adult. I have to find my own way in this world."

"Without money?" he retorted angrily. "You've never taken money seriously. I've always had plenty of it."

Carrie measured the extent of his anger and bewilderment. "I'll be in your debt, Dad. But you have to give me a much wider latitude. With the position I've been offered I have free board and a generous salary. I have Grandma's money, too, if I ever need backup."

"You don't understand," her father said in a near fierce tone. "I don't think I could endure your going away, Carrie. You're the light of my life. My firstborn. Your mother's greatest legacy to me."

Sorrow brushed Carrie's face. "You have another daughter who loves you, Dad, very very much. You have Glenda."

Her father turned his handsome, aggressive head away. "I know and I love them both but my deepest feelings are for *you*, dammit!"

Almost an obsession, Carrie thought. "That's turned us into a triangle, Dad. Me at the top, Glenda and Mel at the sides."

Her answer provoked her father to anger. "I hope your sister has nothing to do with this departure?" he thundered. "A blind man could see how jealous she is of you."

Carrie almost sagged. "Mel has absolutely nothing to

do with it," she told her father resolutely. "I *must* leave, Dad, my own decision. I must be on my own for a while. Mr. McQuillan," she sensed she had better stick to the strictly formal, "will call into the office today to see you. He'll ring beforehand to check if it's convenient."

"Will he now!" Jeff Russell fumed. "I'll see him. I certainly shall. I'm very curious about this McQuillan. He could hire a dozen governesses. Go to an agency. What does he want with you? Glenda tells me he's a divorced man."

Carrie studied her father quietly, feeling love and pity for him. "It happens, Dad. Without it being anyone's fault."

"And he has a child?"

"Of course. Regina will be my charge," she returned levelly.

"It's bloody ridiculous!" Jeff Russell cried in a great burst of agitation. "Trust James to involve himself in all this. Always so gentlemanly but he's always been hostile to me," he sneered. "I believe James is capable of setting this whole thing up. Probably McQuillan has fallen in love with you. You're a very beautiful young woman with lots of fine qualities. I can't imagine for the life of me why he wants to employ you as a governess for his child. I suspect he wants you but he's trying to make it seem respectable. I won't have it!" He jumped up from the table, pushing his chair back so forcibly it scraped along the tiles.

Carrie rose, too, facing her father squarely, something not a lot of people were capable of. "Dad, your estimate of the situation couldn't be more wrong," she said levelly. "Mr. McQuillan is actually being kind to me. He had another type of person in mind. He told me so. I'm the one who pressed for the job. I need to get away from everything to do with my old routine. I need a totally new environment for my feelings of frustration and grief to go away. I beg you to understand. You say you love me...." Abruptly she cracked, tears filling her eyes.

"Carrie, sweetheart!" her father exclaimed, staring back at her in worried perplexity. "You're far more disturbed than I thought. I don't like to see you in this agitated state. It breaks my heart. You need the love and support of your own family, whatever you might think. Perhaps a holiday. Anywhere in the world. Glenda and Melissa can go with you for company. Stay at the best hotels. I should have suggested it long before now."

"I don't want a trip, Dad." She couldn't add, never with Glenda.

"Depression, that's what it is," her father said, his face full of concern. "You don't have to tell me anything about that. I went through hell after your mother died. Hell!" he repeated as though the grief was still too hefty for him to shoulder. "Let me speak to McQuillan. I'm good at sizing men up. Glenda has told me all about his background. Pioneering family and all the rest of it. Chain of cattle stations. That doesn't mean he's the sort of person I want my daughter associating with." Jeff Russell reached out and patted his daughter's shoulder several times. "Leave it to me, Carrie. Leave it to your father. A move away might be all right as long as it's not extended."

Glenda waited until her husband had left, kissing him goodbye in the entrance hall, before she joined Carrie in the morning room where the family had breakfast.

"So how did it go?' she asked, her tone rather brutally avid.

Carrie looked up from where she'd been sitting, looking out at the prolifically flowering garden. Not Glenda's work. They had a wonderful gardener come in three times a week. "My coffee is cold," she said evenly. "Would you like a cup if I make some?"

"I'd like to know what your father had to say?" Glenda answered bluntly.

"Well, let me put your mind at rest." Carrie had already

started to move. "Whatever Dad says, and he doesn't want me to go, I'm accepting the job."

Though Glenda brightened with relief she still managed to sneer, "What job? You must think I'm an idiot if I can't read the signs. You're after him, aren't you?" she said crudely.

"If you think that then you *are* an idiot," Carrie replied, her expression calm and cool.

"That's right, abandon the too-good-to-be-true-golden-girl act." Glenda moved so the two women stood facing each other. "Don't trip up with this one, Carrie," Glenda warned. "I've done my level best for you but it's all gone on far too long. You've cut Melissa off from her own father. You've done everything you could to divert his love from me."

For the first time in her life Carrie felt utterly free of her stepmother. "Oh, come on, Glenda, that's a lie, and you know it." Carrie moved a decisive step forward so the petite Glenda had to fall back. "My father's behaviour is his own. I bent over backward trying to deflect attention from me. And don't kid yourself you did your best for me. You were a rotten caretaker from day one. A woman so mean-spirited you couldn't take a helpless little child into your heart. I could have cared for you but you wouldn't let me. You know my friend Christy Sheppard? She has a stepmother. She adores her. Lucky Christy. Now I'm going to be in the house for a few days more until I can get myself and my things together. I'd advise you—and you'd be wise to observe this to the letter—if you so much as look sideways at me, you or Mel, I'll tell Dad what a rotten bitch you've been to me all these years. And you know what, Glenda? Dad will believe me."

A truth that Glenda recognised with a bitter twist of her mouth.

* * *

Her father drove her out to the airport, smiling through his upset. Whatever Royce McQuillan had said to him, or how he had handled himself, Jeff Russell had settled down from the time of their meeting. He now accepted a complete change of environment on the McQuillan historic station would be in Carrie's best interests.

Royce McQuillan had told him about his family, his grandmother, his uncle Cameron and his wife and his small daughter Regina, all of whom resided at the homestead. Naturally Jeff Russell was happy about that. In fact it was clear to all of them Royce McQuillan had made a decidedly good impression on the notoriously hard-to-please Jeff Russell. It made it possible for Carrie's father to accompany her to the airport and to hug her supportively when she left, telling her if things didn't work out she knew she had a loving home to come back to.

Astute as he was about many things, and Jeff Russell was a very successful businessman, Carrie reflected, her father had been as good as blind as to what went on in his own home.

The thousand-mile flight took her north of Capricorn and into the tropics; over glorious tall green cane country an eternal presence for hundreds of square miles; the great mango plantations, the banana plantations, pawpaws, passionfruit, all manner of exotic new tropical fruits, alongside the Great Barrier Reef, the eighth wonder of the world stretching away out to sea for twelve hundred and fifty miles. As a Queenslander Carrie had visited many beautiful islands of the Reef, swum in the magnificent lagoons, drifted with face mask and snorkel around the submerged coral gardens and hired scuba gear to further explore the incredible beauty of the undersea realm. She'd almost got to the Daintree Rainforest, which joined the turquoise sea, but Melissa had become sick on that particular trip and they had had to return home. Perhaps she would get the opportunity now.

Carrie stared out the porthole at the thick carpet of clouds, marvelling that she was here at all. She'd advised Royce McQuillan by phone she couldn't return with him but needed a few days to ready herself for the trip. As requested she'd faxed him details of her arrival. Either he would drive in from the station to meet her or if he couldn't make it he would send someone, probably his overseer.

The flight was pleasant and uneventful. They landed to brilliant sunshine, the air even brighter, the countryside more densely green and colourful than the subtropical capital. Crimson, white, mauve and orange bougainvillea spilled over fences and pergolas around the airport, the great poincianas were already coming into flower, the tulip trees and the cascara trees lacing their hanging bean pods with yellow bloom. It was much hotter than it had been at home. She was glad she had worn something crisp and fresh, a white cotton and lace shirt with a matching skirt, sandals on her feet. She hadn't forgotten to bring a wide-brimmed hat with her, either, an absolute must anywhere in Queensland with its perpetual sunshine.

A little flushed with excitement, Carrie composed herself to wait. She didn't expect it would be long. Royce McQuillan was very much the sort of man who followed through. The plane had been packed mostly with tourists who used the large coastal town as a jumping off point for the Reef islands, the luxurious Port Douglas resort on the coast or the rainforest. They were waiting now, assembling their luggage, relaxed and carefree, holidays in front of them.

I'm here as a governess, Carrie thought. If anyone had

told me that even a week ago I'd have thought them mad. Her talents such as they now were, lay in a different direction. But she was determined to do a good job. She felt confident about giving Regina lessons, perhaps helping her a great deal. She had been an excellent student herself. Better yet she hoped to make friends with the child, win her confidence and liking. Why not? She'd always got on well with children. In fact she had really enjoyed helping out with students from the Young Conservatorium. But then, she reminded herself, those children were exceptional. They wouldn't have been there otherwise. Regina McQuillan had been labelled "a little terror" by her own father. Albeit he was smiling at the time. The one thing she couldn't be was a failure. She really needed this time out even if Royce McQuillan never spared another minute for her again.

The very strange thing was that nobody came. Not Royce McQuillan. Not anyone from the station. She'd been waiting well over an hour and a half, staring out the window at the landscape. Once she got up to buy herself a Coke. Another plane had arrived, offloading passengers and cargo. She was beginning to feel depressed. Was it possible everyone had forgotten about her? She realised Royce McQuillan would be a very busy man. Perhaps something had gone wrong at the station? Someone had injured themselves? She'd read it happened fairly frequently on Outback stations.

The same female airport attendant who had approached her once before came up to check again if she was all right. It was midafternoon now. Two long slow hours had gone by.

"I was supposed to be met by someone from Maramba Downs," Carrie now explained. "I have to say I'm getting a bit anxious. Would you happen to know the station at all?''

The young woman's face lit up. "Everyone knows Maramba up here. It's one of the best cattle stations in the country. The McQuillan family is big in this part of the world. Something like royalty. You know Royce McQuillan?'' the attendant trilled. Obviously she did.

"I'm here to be governess to his little girl," Carrie told her.

The other young woman squealed. "Boy, you'd have fooled me. You don't look like any governess I've ever seen and I've seen a few passing through."

"Why is that?" Carrie asked, thinking governesses had to be intelligent young women.

"Heavens, you got off the plane like a movie star going incognito.'' The attendant studied her afresh. "Say, why don't you ring the station? Check on whether someone's coming. It's getting pretty late and it's one heck of a drive. A good two hours and that's really movin'.''

"I suppose I'd better." Immediately Carrie stood, looking 'round her.

"I'll keep an eye on your luggage," the young attendant promised. "The phones are over there." She pointed.

"Yes, I know. Thank you." Carrie returned the friendly smile. "Won't be long.''

A woman's voice answered the phone, sounding very, very surprised. "But, my dear, I'm absolutely certain Mr. McQuillan knows nothing about this," the voice informed her. "Why ever didn't you let us know? How very foolish!''

Carrie launched straight into assuring the voice—it turned out to be the housekeeper—she had sent a fax the day before containing all the relevant details.

The upshot of the rather jarring conversation was the housekeeper advised her to take one of the airport buses into town and check into the Paradise Point hotel. Mr. McQuillan would be informed as soon as he came in. The inference plainly was Mr. McQuillan would be displeased and there was a certain amount of dubiousness about whether Carrie had in fact notified the station at all.

"Now, you've got that straight?" the housekeeper double-checked as though Carrie could very well be dim-witted.

"Yes, thank you. The Paradise Point hotel."

"Just tell them you're going on to Maramba Downs," Carrie was further advised. "You won't have to pay for anything."

Carrie hung up, feeling slightly jaundiced. This definitely wasn't a good start. She was highly relieved, too, the housekeeper wasn't a member of the family. She sounded a real dragon.

She watched the tropic sun go down in fiery splendour from the small balcony off her room. They must have thought she was to be a guest of the station because she'd been booked into a room overlooking the sea that was definitely deluxe. Oh, well, if she had to, she'd pay the difference between it and what a station employee would normally rate.

Whatever had happened to her fax? The journal printout on the home office machine had given the OK result, so it must have been received. Yet the housekeeper, her voice saturated in doubt, had given the decided impression all faxes to the station were dealt with promptly. A mystery!

By six-thirty she was starting to get hungry. She'd had a light breakfast at home, keeping out of Glenda's way, no lunch, nothing on the plane. A Coke at the airport terminal. Should she add dinner to the tab? The answer was yes. Royce McQuillan, if she ever saw him again, could dock her wages.

Carrie was running a brush through her hair when there was a knock on the door. She hadn't asked for room service. Maybe they were going to downgrade her to a lower floor. She was determined to make light of this. She put down the brush, glanced at herself briefly in the mirror, then went to open the door.

Like the first moment she'd laid eyes on him she lost time. Royce McQuillan was standing there looking dazzlingly attractive in a khaki shirt, narrow jeans, dusty riding boots on his feet, his black hair glossy as a bird's wing, wind-ruffled into curls, one of which had descended onto his bronze forehead. This was a seriously sexy man.

His very first words, however, were crisp and to the point. "Couldn't you have let us know?"

"I did let you know." She threw him a look of pure censure.

"How?" He surveyed her loftily from head to toe.

She eyed him back, struck afresh by such blazing vitality allied to nonchalant grace. It was even more evident on his home ground, dressed like a cattle man. All he lacked was the big rakish Akubra.

"By fax," she told him, feeling totally connected again. "I can prove it if I have to. At least I think I can. I might have thrown the result slip out. I wanted to leave Dad's study neat."

"You sent a *fax?*" Unexpectedly he lowered his rangy height into the nearest armchair, long legs out in front of him.

"You don't believe me?" She tilted her chin.

His black eyes sparkled like jets. "How can you talk that way when you're supposed to be the governess?" he drawled.

"What way?" She couldn't quite understand him.

"I'm not used to bits of girls tilting their chin at me," he explained.

"Right. I'll stare at the floor." Hadn't she first thought his employees would address him staring at his feet? "I'm so sorry you didn't get my message. I did send it. Perhaps it's been missed."

"Nope." He ran a hand over his dashing black head. "I believe every last fax has been checked."

"Then I don't understand." Carrie gestured a little wanly.

"Me, either. Anyway I'm here."

"You drove in?" And it was such a trek she'd been told.

"I didn't *fly*," he said dryly. "It's a long drive but too short to take up a plane."

"How kind of you," she murmured sweetly into the pause.

"Isn't it? I'm damned hungry. It was one hell of a day. Have you eaten?"

Carrie shook her head. "I was just about to commit a mortal sin and put dinner on the tab."

He laughed as though she amused him. "I have to wash up." He got to his feet, waves of pure energy coming off every movement. "We'll stay the night and travel back first thing in the morning. Suit you?"

"Whatever suits *you,* Mr. McQuillan." It was not said provocatively yet little lights sprang into his eyes.

"It was Royce the other night," he retaliated, rolling his own name off his tongue.

"This is different," she pointed out. "You're my boss now."

"Well, I don't care. As long as it's all right with *me* you can keep on calling me Royce."

"With a title perhaps? Mr. Royce?"

He shot her a slow, admonishing look. "Okay, have fun, Catrina. I may yet call you Cat. You have claws." At the door he turned. "I won't keep you waiting long. Give me twenty minutes. I booked a table when I came in. A lot of monied tourists are in town.''

I've only known him a handful of hours and already I'm in too deep, Carrie thought, torn between excitement and dismay.

When they walked into the dining room people nodded and waved from all directions. Obviously he was very well known. In fact it appeared when he was in town he was the hotel's number one diner. Curious eyes flickered over Carrie. Men and women, prompting her to say governesses didn't normally get invited out to dinner.

"You're not invited out," he said, one black brow arched. "You just happen to be here and you're hungry. You're also the one who got me to drive in hell-for-leather after a long hard day. I really should have sent you off to bed without dinner.''

"I'm glad you didn't.'' She blushed.

"What were you thinking all the hours you were waiting?'' He lifted his eyes from the menu to ask.

"Life is never meant to be easy,'' she said sweetly.

He laughed beneath his breath. "I wonder if I can get you to sample one of this restaurant's best dishes?''

"Not kangaroo. Please not kangaroo,'' she begged.

"You wouldn't know what you were eating if I didn't tell you.''

"But I do trust you to tell me. I guess it has to be crocodile?'' Her amber eyes sparkled.

"How clever of you, Catrina. There's a marvellous tian of smoked crocodile and corn-fed chicken on the menu served with a lettuce leaf mixture, diced apple and avocado in a dressing topped off with tomato coulis. You could have that as an entré.''

"Sorry, I'm going to have the crab and paw paw salad,'' she murmured. "And seeing I'm in cattle country privi-

leged to be dining with the local cattle king, I should try
the beef tenderloin with red wine shallot sauce and sautéed
mushrooms.''

"I'm pleased you said that, Catrina,'' Royce cautioned.
"It's all Maramba beef.''

Afterward they went for a short stroll along the seafront,
the water glimmering with luminescence, a drench of
sweetness from the flowering shrubs, a heavenly sea breeze
blowing, setting the fronds of the great palms in motion,
seductive pockets of shadow that filtered out the street-
lights. It was bliss after the brilliant glare of the day, the
starry fastness of the night sky so beautiful it made Carrie
ache to see it. She realised with a profound sense of shock
from the moment Royce McQuillan had come into her life
her internal focusing had shifted. Her preoccupation with
him had set up some kind of a pain barrier. She had
stopped thinking about her accident or what it had done to
her life carrying her from a peak into a deep trough.
Instead she was thinking almost exclusively about him.
About how women fell madly in love with certain men.
What was it about, then? Their overwhelming masculinity?
Their physical beauty? Virility? Their toughness, their lean
hard bodies as compared to a woman's soft yielding satin
flesh?

There was a real buzz about this man. Like electricity
in the air. Sex appeal, they called it. He had it in abun-
dance. Yet his marriage hadn't worked out. She had seen
his handsome face set in sombre lines when he spoke about
it. She had seen the glitter of obsession in his ex-wife's
ice-blue eyes. Carrie just knew Sharon McQuillan would
come back into the picture. At least there was no bitter
struggle for custody of Regina. Peculiar as it was, Sharon
McQuillan, according to her ex-husband, had never wanted

her own child. It was one of those things that happened occasionally, leaving anguish in its wake.

They walked in harmony, hardly talking, each ostensibly enjoying the night, yet deep down intensely aware of each other. Feelings were gathering like a storm. Each realised this sudden violent attraction that had sprung up between them had to be crushed. Yet to Carrie it seemed as though the world had changed. She felt slightly wild, out of control, yet ready to sheer off like the cat he had called her.

"I suppose we'd better go back," Royce murmured eventually as they came to a small resting point along the promenade, the water lapping peacefully. "Fairly early start in the morning. I won't get you up at dawn but you should set your alarm for six, with breakfast at six-thirty. Ring room service. We'll take off after that. I have a couple of buyers flying in the afternoon. I have to be there."

"Your uncle couldn't handle it?" she asked, wondering how much he delegated.

"Better if I'm there," he said briefly, a touch of his hand turning her.

They were a short distance from the hotel, walking out from beneath a huge poinciana surrounded by a bed of cool ferns, when a lone flying fox on its nocturnal haunt all but dive-bombed them flapping its leathery wings. It shrieked so strangely for a moment, Carrie who was well used to the sight and familiar whirring sound of fruit bats invading their own fruit trees, scarcely knew what manner of bird it was. But it was as aggressive as a nesting magpie.

"There's one bat looking for trouble," Royce rasped, one arm around Carrie who had her head bent to protect her face, the other still holding the long twig he had snatched up as a defensive weapon.

"Maybe it just got lost?" Carrie's voice quavered, almost drowning in sensation having him so overpoweringly close.

"The damn thing was huge!" He sounded both amused and outraged. "You're okay, aren't you?"

When every muscle, every sinew, was twitching under her treacherous skin. "Of course I am!"

Yet she was as poised and alert as a dancer, he thought, ready to spring away across a stage. The breeze had begun to play with her hair, skeining it like a cloud of silk across his cheek. Perfumed, buoyant, so soft and warm. He caught a handful in his fist, relishing the texture. Her slender form was wedged against his hip, alluringly female. Shining skin so beautiful it begged to be touched.

God, this was madness, he thought, trying to abide by common sense. It had taken him too long to get control of life to fall into the labyrinth again. Catrina Russell, the new governess. Poised and controlled one moment, a panicked little girl the next. He was half horrified by the extent of his own desire. It was unimaginable the way it had all happened. Outside forces ruling one's life.

She straightened, trying to joke. "I'm sorry, you must think me a real cream puff."

"Ice cream," he corrected with a self-mocking half laugh. "Vanilla and apricot." He could taste her soft mouth against his. The upper lip was finely cut, the lower enticingly full. Her body was in silhouette as the darkness beneath another poinciana deepened. She was increasing her speed, long lovely legs moving easily over the ground, carrying her away from him. "No need to apologise, Catrina," he called after her dryly, "the damn thing startled me, too."

She paused beneath a streetlight, her hair billowing, doubled by the breeze into a gleaming mane so it resembled a bright satin cloak haloing her face. Her eyes had a glittery look to them and her cheeks were darkened with blood. She had a high mettled look to her, a capacity for passion she must bring to her music. He could imagine what she would be like under his hand....

When he reached her he was so moved by her beauty he pulled her into his arms, wondering if his life was ever going to be normal again. Desire was like an avalanche thundering down a mountain. You couldn't get out of the way. Acutely aware of her *stillness,* her intoxicating fragrance all around him, he all but seized her up, his breathing a little harsh. "Maybe if we get this over, we can settle down," he suggested with acid self-mockery.

Boundless excitement spread rapidly all over her body, flooding her. She felt dizzy with shock and unbearable tension, her open mouth soft and vulnerable, waiting for his as though her body was in sole charge and her mind had gone numb. In her whole life for all her small triumphs on the concert stage there was nothing to measure against this. This excitement was so extreme.

He drew her back into the shadows, shifting her weight onto his heart, taking her mouth in a kiss that went on...and on...and on...the most ravishing invasion, Carrie totally submissive as though forbidden fruit was all the sweeter. He kissed her until her wildly beating heart was ready to explode, then he released her from the spell, his dark vibrant voice bizarrely normal, even conversational.

"We both wanted that, Catrina," he said briskly, "even if it might have been the worst thing I could have done. If it's any consolation, I promise it won't happen again."

She was shaken to the core, but years of conquering nerves stood her in good stead. "Which is a blessing," she managed calmly even if her voice was very soft. "I really don't think I could handle it."

"Me, either," he said smoothly, still trying to analyse his complex feelings. Kissing her was akin to a storm blowing up inside him. It had taken every ounce of his self-control to let her go, when he couldn't get enough of her. Something so dangerous he instinctively had to step back from it. He thought of her vulnerability at this time when she was attempting to build a new life for herself. It would be callous to threaten her further.

Carrie didn't have to rely on an alarm as a safety net. Dawn cracked open to frantic birdsong, sweet, melancholy, warbling, the reckless cackle of the blue-winged kooka-burras in the trees beneath her room. It was impossible to go back to sleep, though her night had been disturbed by broken dreams. Her subconscious was so in thrall, Royce McQuillan had figured in them all, his presence so deliriously strong at one time she awoke heart thudding, thinking he was in the bed with her, his hand on her breast. Small wonder she felt too keyed up to eat much break-fast—orange juice, tropical fruit salad, coffee—but she was dressed and waiting when he knocked on her door.

"All set?"

She was almost relieved to see his brilliant gaze was impersonal as it ran over her, checking out her attire for the long trip. She had dressed coolly but sensibly in a navy T-shirt with a designer label worked into the front, white cotton jeans, and navy sneakers. Because of the heat, she had caught her hair back into a gold clasp at the nape. She followed his cue, speaking as though not one moment of passionate intensity had passed between them. "I hope I didn't bring too much luggage?" She indicated the three pieces.

"Does a princess take too much luggage?" He pretended to lift one of her suitcases with difficulty.

"I can take one." She wanted to be helpful.

"That's a relief!" His mouth quirked. He was determined to start the day off lightly. Cut the fuse that ran directly to dynamite. "No, I can manage, Catrina," he told her casually. "We don't need to bother with room service.

You've only got the three pieces. I'll tuck one under my arm.''

She watched him, as he went about doing it, his movements lithe and economical, while he told her to leave the keys on the small circular table and the door open. He'd settled the bill the night before.

"I hope you've got a wide-brimmed hat?" he paused to ask.

"Of course." She reached behind her for the straw hat lying on the bed.

"Plenty of sunscreen?"

"Never leave home without it. Believe it or not, I don't burn."

"Let's keep it that way," he said briefly, his striking face as calm and inscrutable as a mask.

Ten minutes later they were underway, driving out of the large prosperous town and picking up the main highway, Carrie in the passenger seat of the Range Rover, Royce behind the wheel. At this hour the heat of the day was diffused, the morning incandescent. Open savannahs rolled away from the highway to the range, the lush green strip of coastline overlooking a sea ablaze in blues, ultramarines, cerulean, turquoise, cobalt.

"Do you mind if I put the window down?" she asked a few miles on.

"You don't get car sick do you?" He glanced at her. "Or does the air conditioning bother you?"

"Neither. I wanted to smell the bush. I love the way the sun warms the leaves on the gums! It releases the most marvellous aroma."

"It's the distinctive scent of the Australian bush." He lowered his own window only a short way so he wouldn't create a cross draft, letting in the fragrance of the flowing morning. Across the grasslands, Carrie glimpsed kangaroos bounding as silently as spirits into the shade of the

trees. Their benign presence gave her such a warm feeling.
The Range Rover was moving smoothly at speed, on the
two-hour journey that would take them into the heart of
Maramba. Once an emu paced the 4WD showing a short
but fantastic turn of speed—60 m.p.h., Royce told her.

All along the route Carrie was fascinated by the towering purple and cerise banks of bougainvillea gone wild.
It rose like brilliantly coloured ramparts to either side of
the highway. A veritable jungle with those dangerous
hooked thorns, but magnificently showy. In the gardens at
home a whole range of cultivars thrived, the Thai golds,
the hot pinks, the scarlets, the bronzes and burnt oranges,
showy and relatively easy to handle, but they never at-
tained the incredible height and splendour of their bush
cousins. Away to the west rose the ragged peaks of the
Great Diving Range, mauvish purple against the cloudless
deep blue sky.

"They really do look like larkspur," Carrie observed,
harking back to a famous Australian poem listing the beau-
ties of the homeland.

"At this time of day," he agreed. "Later on they turn
to grape. The truly spectacular changes occur in the Red
Centre. I don't think any other region can rival it, glorious
as our tropics are. Those uncompromising ochres. The pri-
meval beauty. You've been to Ulura and the Olgas?"

She shook her head regretfully. "Even to an Australian
it's *so* far away! I've been studying most of my life. There
has never been time. But I would adore to go."

"Then you might make it," he surprised her by saying
casually. "We have stations all over. From the Channel
Country in the far southwest up to the Gulf of Carpentaria.
Jimboola in the Channel Country would be the best jumping off point. I fly down fairly frequently. You can come
with me for the trip. But in the months ahead it's going to
get damned hot. You could very well melt away."

"I won't. I know how to keep my cool."

His white smile gleamed. "I've noticed that." He made a brief gesture toward the ever-present ranges that rose like a great barrier between the verdant benevolent coastal strip and the sun-scorched vast inland. "The most dominating geographical feature of our continent," he pointed out, "rambling way down the eastern seaboard, some 500 kilometres. From the tropical tip of our own state of Queensland, through rain forest, semi-desert, snowy alps and beautiful pastoral country to end in the Victorian Grampians two states away."

Carrie saw it, as it must have been. "A very frightening and daunting obstacle to the first settlers in Sydney," Carrie said.

"Twenty-four years to cross the Blue Mountains and open the great western plains to the infant colony. What Blaxland Lawson and Wentworth must have looked out on? In any man's language, the Promised Land. The pastoralists lost no time taking up their grand selections. My own family included. The first McQuillan to arrive in Australia was one James Alastair McQuillan who arrived in the colony with his wife Catriona—which is one reason I like to call you Catrina—and their two young children. That was Christmas 1801. They must have nearly died of the heat after Scotland. James, a younger son, was the only member of the McQuillan family to come to the new colony. He wanted to make his fortune. And he did. From all accounts he was very friendly with Governor Macquarie. Anyway he was granted a big parcel of land outside Sydney at Parramatta. The old homestead is still there, very well looked after, incidentally, by the family who took it over some hundred years later. James' son, Bruce, had a difficult and strained relationship with his father. He migrated to Queensland in the mid-1800's. James himself was killed in a shootout with a band of escaped convicts.

"How terrible!" Carrie was a little shaken by the thought.

He shrugged. "I don't think James McQuillan, though a 'gentleman' and a free settler, would have been classed as a kindly man. Desperate times produce desperate men. I can't help feeling sorry for a whole class of so-called 'convicts.' Poverty and starvation begets all sorts of crimes. Ferocious cruelties play a big part. The brute with the whip, savage guards, harsh overseers on pastoral properties. Some sixty percent of the convicts who were sent out here had never before committed a crime. And such crimes! Petty theft. Stealing a loaf of bread. Apples from over a wall. Poaching a rabbit from some rich landowner. Theft of any kind was always punished by transportation. Those crimes would hardly earn a fine in today's society, but criminal law in Georgian England was brutal.

"Then there was the wave of 'political' and 'agricultural protester' crimes. The 'utterings' in the streets, voices raised against the government. The dissidents quickly found themselves transported. The irony is as an English historian pointed out, the worst criminals remained in England while a whole class of 'victims' men, women and children, suffered being torn from their country, their families and sent to our wild shores. No wonder the ones who survived were tough. Many of the emancipists, the risen convicts, became very powerful and wealthy with immense land holdings."

"Yes, I know. It's an extraordinary story," Carrie agreed. "My own family on both sides hailed from England. Strangely they all migrated at the same time. After World War I. The men had fought in France and managed to survive. They and their wives decided they wanted to get as far away from Europe as they could."

"Then Australia would have done it," he said dryly.

"So the only one hundred per cent Australians are the

Aborigines," Carrie said, definitely sympathetic to the aboriginal displacement.

"The historic custodians of our land. Nowhere on the continent do you feel their 'presence,' their Dreamtime culture, more strongly than at the Red Centre. When I take you there, you'll know what I mean."

"I'm astonished at your continuing kindness." She smiled. "Meanwhile we're in the glorious tropics. It has its own unique characters."

He made a little sound of agreement. "Brilliant skies, brilliant sea, brilliant landscapes. The dazzling light more than anything. The heightening of the senses. The most spectacular time is on the verge of the Wet that will come up in a month or so. The Wet brings the bush to flower. It brings cyclones, too. The big heat and humidity when you just want to sit with an ice-cold beer in one hand staring out over the garden. I never seem to get the chance. Do you ride, by the way?" he asked, suddenly serious.

"I haven't done for a couple of years but I was taught properly. Dad saw to that. All of the children I knew, all my friends, belonged to a pony club."

"Well, at least that's off my mind!" He gave a low laugh. "The Australian love affair with horses. They've played such a role in opening up this country, especially the Outback. At one time I was pretty serious about joining the Australian Olympic team. The team Three Day Event and Show Jumping. I'd won a few trophies. I was good. I'd received a few approaches. That was when my father was alive and expected to go on living to a ripe old age. It didn't happen," he said grimly, "neither did my Olympic dream. I play polo. We all do and we still use horses to work our cattle. When anyone says horses are stupid creatures I see red. A horse's courage and intelligence has saved many a stockman's life. Horses are our mates in the Outback."

"You won't get any argument from me," Carrie reassured him. "They're magnificent creatures. I cried when our Three Day Event team won their third consecutive gold at the 2000 Olympics. Our horsemen are marvellous when it's tough, dangerous, going. As a complete contrast, I loved the horses performing to music in the dressage section. Responding to all those signals. If that's not high intelligence, what is?"

"I agree." He nodded. "So many who performed brilliantly. I was actually there in Sydney to congratulate Andrew Hoy and other members of the team. It's still in my blood. I stayed for the pool and the equestrian events then I had to head back home."

"Lucky you!" Carrie said lightly. "The TV coverage had to do me. It was wonderful."

The miles flew and the talk became animated as they relived the Olympic experience.

"So it wasn't *all* half crazy with grief over the loss of your career?" he asked eventually.

"Whole hours out," she admitted, "with my accident forgotten. Those horrible moments when I knew we were about to crash. I even knew I was going to get hurt in a way that would affect my life."

"Then it's a bit of serious experimentation, isn't it, being a governess?" He swung his head. "I've transported you out of your sheltered environment into the wild bush. Maramba, though, it doesn't suffer anything like the isolation of Jimboola in the Channel Country or another outstation of ours up in the Gulf in crocodile country, is cut right off from all the excitements and activities of city life. You'll be starved of a lot of things you've got used to."

"I'll cope," she said briefly.

"You'll have to," he told her bluntly. "I'm a very busy man. I wouldn't know how to act nursemaid."

"Nursemaid! Heavens, I'm not going to bother you," Catrina protested.

He didn't try to hide his concern. "Regina is a great little kid. A real survivor, but like I told you, she's a fair terror. She has a really worrying trick of hiding. She can find places no one including me has ever thought of. I *cannot*," he emphasised, "do this baby-sitting thing. My grandmother suffers badly from arthritis. Some days she's in a great deal of pain. We have a good aboriginal woman called Jada, married to our leading stockman, who looks after my grandmother's needs. She's like a personal maid but much closer, more family. She was born on the station. Neither can help out with Regina. My uncle's wife has no great feeling for children. She doesn't want children herself. Regina's mother is, as I told you, a write-off. Our housekeeper, Mrs. Gainsford, runs the homestead like a five-star general. She's super-efficient if not kind and cuddly. She does her best to control Regina's little excesses of temperament but she can be a touch stern. Needless to say she and Regina don't hit it off."

"She wasn't too sweet to me, either," Carrie said dryly.

"You mean she didn't believe you'd sent word?"

"That's what I mean."

"I expect Regina nicked it just for the hell of it," he suggested wryly.

"She's old enough to check the faxes and take mine in?" Carried asked in surprise.

He groaned. "Regina is six going on six hundred," he said. "An *old* soul. I care about her very much."

Although the tone was deeply sincere to Carrie's ears it sounded a shade odd. "I would think so," she said. "Who better than a father to love his daughter?"

"You would know," he said, still with that undercurrent in his tone. "Anyway, you're the boss. She's a dreadful eater by the way."

"That's it. Give it all to me now," Carrie crowed.

"Pecks at everything like a budgie. Has numerous hates. Throws things all over the place. Is very wilful. Always makes a drama of mealtime. Otherwise she's a great kid."

Carrie was undismayed. This was a child, after all, and a child in need of love and understanding. "I'll just have to work out what she likes." She spoke simply. "One thing I wanted to ask you?" She turned her head to look at him, struck by the bronzed glow of his skin, the inky blackness of his well-shaped brows.

"Fire away!" He gave her a brief brilliant glance.

"Did you tell anyone about my background?" she asked quietly. "The fact I was going to New York to study. My accident?"

"My grandmother only," he told her. "It was told to her in confidence. She will respect it. Whatever you wish to do, Catrina, is up to you. All the rest of the family was told you were handpicked by my trusted solicitor."

"Good. I don't want to talk about my accident," Carrie said. "You do understand?"

"Whatever makes you happy," he responded almost gently. "*For now*. One day you're going to have to talk it out. I know about bitter disappointments, Catrina, I can spare you the time."

CHAPTER FIVE

MARAMBA Downs, taken up by Bruce McQuillan in the 1870s, started its huge run on the coast and ran in a north-westerly direction right up to the thickly wooded slopes of the Great Dividing Range. Driving through it, Carrie thought she had never seen more exotically beautiful country in her life. The sparkling clarity of the air rendered more brilliant the full palette of colours. The mountain ranges formed a backdrop, the turquoise sea to the east, the offshore islands and the Great Barrier Reef beyond, immediately inland superb grasslands; endless lush pastures of blue and green grasses with sleek Brahmin cattle grazing alongside prolific birdlife.

On the many lagoons Carrie was enchanted to see great flocks of swans, pelicans, ducks, the entrancing blue brolgas, the huge jabirus, the biggest bird in Australia, and flights of magpie geese that had ruined the rice industry in the tropical north to the extent not even the manoeuvres of the Australian Air Force could deter their attacks on the crop. In one pond white ibis had staked total claim, probing the bottom of the emerald pool with their long beaks, the surface laced with pink and white waterlilies. The atmosphere was so peaceful, so open, so free, she could literally breathe it in.

As they drove further into the heart of the station a large flight of birds suddenly rose from the waters, numerous in the air, the Royal Spoonbills she could identify and concentrations of ducks with very pretty pale yellow plumes. She was about to ask Royce McQuillan their name when he spoke.

93

"Outbuildings coming up." He lifted an indicating hand from the wheel. "The hangars and landing strip off to the right. One for the Beech Baron, the other for our two helicopters. We use them for musters and other purposes. The landing strip is all-weather, as it would have to be when we get the rains. There's a building for just about everything. Freezing rooms, machinery, equipment, tack, saddles. We cure and tan our own leather. It's important to have materials on hand for repair. Staff bungalows and bunkhouses on this side." He indicated again. "The building with the blue roof is the gym and entertainment centre when the men can relax. You might think they get enough hard work in the saddle but they like working out. You won't see the homestead until we're almost upon it. The home gardens in some places have turned into a jungle. I'll have to have it cleared. It's almost a rainforest. Near the house it's more open woodland. We don't want snakes in the house but I have to warn you, you're going to see a few. The thing to remember is snakes do their level best to keep out of our way. Of course if you're unlucky to stand on one...." He shrugged expressively.

"I'll watch where I put my feet," Carrie guaranteed.

The outbuildings behind them, Royce drove more slowly, pointing out different features. "We're in the home gardens now."

Carrie was silent for a moment, thinking it was more like an enchanted forest than a garden. She stared out the window, transfixed by the extent of it, and the great diversity of vegetation. Palms towered, staghorns and elkhorns of incredible size were affixed to the great shade trees, tropical orchids quivered in the breeze, yellow, palest green, pure white, the rich purple of the Cooktown orchid, the state emblem. There were flowery shrubs of all kinds, hardy bromeliads, agaves and aloes, gorgeously coloured beds of foliage to rival the dense green and cascading everywhere flowering vines in every conceivable colour, the bright violet-blue of the morning glories, the pink, white, scarlet, orange and sunshine yellow of the trumpet flowers.

As she continued to look, the curving drive became straight, now it was lined on either side by sentinel Cuban Royals, their fronds moving above the shadowy canopy of the giant shade trees, the poincianas. It would be paradise when those trees broke out, Carrie thought. There were so many of them they would colour the very air.

Almost before she was aware of it the homestead rose up.

It was *huge!* Even bigger than she had envisioned from the photograph Melissa had shown her. A tropical mansion constructed of dark timbers, to meld perfectly with the environment. The building was two-storied, with great wrap-around verandahs on all sides, at least twelve feet in depth, she gauged, the roofline dipping protectively over it like a great shady hat. It was enormously impressive. Enormously picturesque. Just as in the photographs, a lagoon lay at the homestead's feet ringed by all manner of tall water grasses and aquatic plants, sections of it floating the blue lotus, sacred flower of ancient Egypt, native to both Australia and North Africa. There was even a small boat amid the reeds.

"What a wonderful place to live," she exclaimed. "It's like something out of a Somerset Maugham story." She loved the way the landscape flowed toward the house. Massive in anyone's language, there had been minimal impact on the site.

He glanced at her, well pleased by her reaction. "That was the intention, Catrina. This isn't the original homestead, by the way. That was destroyed in a cyclone many years ago. This one is cyclone-proof. *We hope.* My grandfather built it. He'd travelled widely in South East Asia. You'll see the influences, outside and in."

"Your own private kingdom," she marvelled.

"It is." There was pride in his voice, but an unmistakeable thread of grief. "But no man has complete control over life. Over nature. This may look like a man's dream but life isn't. Dreams as we both know can be very easily shattered."

They arrived to a situation. Regina had gone missing, Royce was informed the moment he set foot on the verandah.

Mrs. Gainsford, a tall thin woman, thin face, thin body, thin voice, but looking decidedly frazzled, attempted to explain, standing there, hands folded, awaiting some kind of judgement. Never once did she look in Carrie's direction. No, it was the "master" who was the only one of importance.

"I've done everything in my power, Mr. McQuillan, to see that Regina was here when you arrived," she burst out. "In fact I was congratulating myself I had won the battle. It wasn't until a half hour ago I realised Regina was nowhere in the house. Or nowhere I know about. It makes me look so foolish, so ineffective," she concluded hotly, ready to put the blame on a six-year-old.

"Try to forget about it," Royce McQuillan advised sardonically. "I know you do your best, Mrs. Gainsford." He turned to Carrie. "This is our new governess, Catrina Russell. She'll be responsible for Regina in future."

"Splendid!" the housekeeper clipped off, her expression conveying she didn't believe for a moment Carrie would succeed where she couldn't. "I have your room ready, I'll show you to it."

"Thank you." Carrie offered a smile before addressing Royce McQuillan directly. "Where do you suggest I might look for Regg... Regina?" She almost slipped and said Reggie. She had come to think of this little "terror" as Reggie.

"She'll come out when she's good and ready," he said wryly. "Regina needs to make a statement more than most. Of course if she hasn't shown herself by lunchtime we'll have to organise a little search party."

"She never touched a bite of breakfast, either," Mrs. Gainsford broke in, looking like this was yet another grave offence. "I'm *so* sorry, Mr. McQuillan. I simply dread what more shocks Regina has in store for us."

Perhaps it wasn't the right moment but Carrie burst out laughing. A laugh she quickly snuffed at the cold stare in her direction. This was a woman she would have to work with, Carrie thought, though she had the decided feeling she and Mrs. Gainsford would never be onside.

"And where's Mrs. McQuillan?" Royce was asking the housekeeper rather pointedly, giving Carrie quite a chill. For a moment she thought he meant his wife.

"Here, Royce!" a voice called, heavy with overtones. As though she had been watching, waiting in the wings, a striking-looking woman in her mid to late thirties with short, thick, smartly cropped fair hair, tanned skin and very bright blue eyes appeared, offering the master of the house a strangely provocative smile. "I wanted to be here the moment you arrived but I've been looking for Regina. Not that any of us can stop her when she wants to hide. And this, I take it, is the new governess?" The electric-blue gaze moved to Carrie.

Just a wee bit….astonished? Definitely not friendly. Expect no support there, Carrie thought. An element of the furious look Sharon McQuillan had given her.

"My dear, you couldn't have arrived at a better time," this striking woman said, stalking forward on sandals with very high heels. At the last moment she paused beside Royce McQuillan, lifted her head and gave him a kiss on the cheek that lingered far too long. "Welcome home, Royce, I've missed you."

He glanced down into her upturned face. "What in a matter of hours?"

To Carrie's acute ears the tone was cutting, but Lindsey McQuillan—it had to be—appeared to revel in it.

He made to introduce them and Carrie found herself subjected to an even more intense scrutiny.

"I gather James Halliday recommended you for the job?" Lindsey McQuillan asked as though she was about to make notes. "I never did hear your exact qualifications?"

Carrie wasn't flustered although it looked very much like Mrs. Lindsey McQuillan had taken a dislike to her on sight.

"They're adequate, Mrs. McQuillan," she said courteously.

"Well, we'll see." The other woman stared back as though she didn't want to leave it there. "Regina's governesses haven't done so well in the past."

"Maybe you had something to do with that, Lyn," Royce McQuillan tossed her way. "I'm hoping you'll give Catrina your support."

"Oh, I will. I will. Quite rightly." She smiled back at him in that ominous intimate way, when she might have said, Not me! I haven't got the energy. "Anything you want to know you must come to me." She eyed the label on Carrie's expensive T-shirt and didn't appear comfortable with it.

Carrie obliged her with a thank you.

"Where's Gran?" Royce suddenly asked, sounding to Carrie's ears as though he didn't want to leave her alone with his glamorous "aunt."

"Resting," Mrs. Gainsford supplied as Lindsey McQuillan held back from an answer. "It's not one of her good days, but she'll be wanting to meet the young lady later on."

"Well, Carrie, I'll leave you to get settled." Royce gave her a bracing glance. "I have things to do."

"Fine. I'll be fine."

Carrie's assurances were all but drowned by Lindsey McQuillan's cry of dismay. "But surely you've got time for a cup of coffee, Royce? I want to tell you all about a phone call I had from Ina."

Immediately his face hardened. "It'll keep. If Regina doesn't show up in an hour or so, get word to me. I see Arundi working around the grounds. He can take one of the Jeeps. I'll be at the Four Mile. Cam's there, isn't he?" he asked Lindsey with a twist of his raven head.

"I expect so," she answered languidly. "He's where you told him to be, Royce, darling. *Naturally.*"

Royce McQuillan moved off. They heard his voice outside telling someone to take Carrie's luggage into the house.

"Come this way, Miss Russell," the housekeeper said.

"Carrie, please," Carrie suggested pleasantly.

Mrs. Gainsford scorned that. "I prefer to call you Miss Russell, if you don't mind."

"Makes me seem too much of a personage." Carrie smiled.

"You'll have to be something of a personage to keep Regina under control," the housekeeper said with a tight mouth. "No mother! It's showing dreadfully. Mr. McQuillan is a wonderful man. A very important man. He shouldn't have all this worry on his mind."

"I expect you spare him a lot with your competence." Carrie offered an olive branch. "He told me you ran the homestead splendidly."

That brought an instant reaction. A dark red flush and a complete softening of the rather harsh face with a smile. "Did he now?"

"Certainly. He must greatly appreciate having the house run so efficiently."

"A perfect gentleman he is!" Mrs. Gainsford put real feeling into her voice. "A perfect gentleman. It's a wonder to work for someone like that."

Carrie couldn't help but agree.

The room she had been allotted was much more than Carrie had expected. In scale with the rest of the house it was huge. Maybe three times the size of her bedroom at home. Here was the Asian influence Royce McQuillan had spoken about. Thai, she considered thoughtfully. The family had holidayed in Bali several times. A marvellous teak bed occupied centre room, slender four posters holding up the billowing folds of the white mosquito netting, edged top and bottom with heavy white embroidery that matched the white bed linen. There were two carved teak chairs and a small matching table with an eye-catching floral arrangement on top. A comfortable day bed was near the window with an Oriental chest at the foot of the bed. There was a teak cabinet holding a collection of Chinese blue and white porcelain, a deep comfortable armchair upholstered in white Indian cotton, an ottoman with a brilliant throw across it, an Indian-style carved armoire in one corner, and a tall bookcase filled with books in another. She caught a few names: Isabel Allende, Sharon Maas, P.D. James, Kathy Reichs.... On one wall was a brilliant painting executed in oils of outsize golden sunflowers surrounded by colourful foliage set against a cobalt sky.

"Oh, I'm going to love staying here," she said, her topaz eyes full of pleasure.

"I'm not surprised!" Mrs. Gainsford sniffed audibly. "No other governess has been given such a room. But Mr. McQuillan gave orders."

"Aren't I lucky!" Carrie moved across the polished floor decorated with a single exquisite Oriental rug.

"You are indeed," Mrs. Gainsford pronounced, back to her reedy tone. "There are some really valuable things in here. All that embroidery on the bed linen was done by hand, you know."

"It's lovely. I'll look after it."

"I change the bedding twice a week. One of my girls will do the cleaning. You don't have any chores to take up your time."

"Thank you for making it so welcoming for me," Carrie said, giving the older woman a happy smile. "The flower arrangement is quite beautiful."

Mrs. Gainsford glanced toward the teak table where the rich red of anthurium lilies glowed against three large dark green leaves, a piece of strangler vine to one side, a burst of grevillea to the other. It was a most unusual arrangement, perfect in its ceramic container with what appeared to be aboriginal motifs.

"Jada did that," the housekeeper said without enthusiasm. "She thought you might like it. I prefer a good straightforward bunch of flowers any day, but Mr. McQuillan allows Jada do the flowers for the house. Keeps her busy when she's not attending to Mrs. McQuillan senior."

"I'm so sorry Mrs. McQuillan isn't well," Carrie said carefully.

"A marvellous lady! Never complains. She said something about seeing you when you're settled. I'll let you know. Meanwhile we've got no other option but to wait for Miss Regina to appear. More than anything else she needs discipline that child."

And a mother's love. If there was anything about Royce McQuillan Carrie might have criticized it was his casual attitude to his little daughter. Couldn't he have said, I love her deeply, rather than I really care about her. Even Uncle James told her frequently how much he loved her. Yet

Royce McQuillan had used the word "cared." There was a good chance Regina wasn't getting enough love from him, Carrie thought.

Mrs. Gainsford went to the door; turning to tell Carrie a light lunch would be served at 1:00 p.m. Meanwhile she was free to settle in and have a rest after her trip. "I expect you've done quite a bit of travelling in the last couple of days."

"Some," Carrie smiled. "You never did find my fax?"

"I apologise if I ever doubted you," the housekeeper said abruptly. "You look a responsible young woman. It was Regina for sure. She's always doing silly things. Now I must be off. You should rest now."

"I'm sure I won't be able to nod off without knowing where Regina is," Carrie said.

"No chance of your finding her if she doesn't want to be found," Mrs. Gainsford said, frown lines forming between her sparse brows. "I wouldn't have thought she had the brain power to get up to the things she does. She's a *child,* yet she gives as much trouble as a woman."

"I hope Regina and I are going to be good friends," Carrie said quietly.

"Then, my dear, you're hoping a lot. This is no little sweetheart you'll be dealing with. This is an exceptionally naughty girl."

Again Carrie felt like laughing out loud. Such a very capable woman to be outplayed by a six-year-old. It reminded her of the way Glenda used to call her "an uncontrollable child."

With the housekeeper gone Carrie wandered out onto the verandah, looking down its long length. Golden canes in huge pots glazed a deep bronze were set at intervals at either side of the pairs of French doors. She couldn't wait to see over the house. The entrance hall was enormous, the soaring ceiling the full height of the building with two broad staircases leading off on either side to the upper gallery that ran right around the second floor. Asian influences appeared to be everywhere. She had taken that in at a glance. This was a marvellous tropical house.

She was humming quietly to herself, unpacking the luggage a gently spoken aboriginal man had brought to her door only a few minutes before. He had introduced himself as Arundi. The same Arundi who had to carry word to Royce McQuillan if Regina didn't surface by lunchtime. Carrie just hoped she would. She really wanted to meet Miss Regina McQuillan.

No way did she imagine Regina would be in the armoire.

Carrie's heart leapt in shock as she opened the carved door. She had, in passing, noted it wasn't quite closed, but never did she expect a small girl to confront her, all thin arms and legs, pulling a ferocious face, no doubt meant to be frightening.

Carrie had to wait a full minute before she could talk. "Heavens, Reggie, you scared the life out of me."

"That's great!" the little girl responded triumphantly. "No one *ever* looks for me in the right place."

"You mean, you were here all along?" Carrie wasn't happy about what Mrs. Gainsford had said.

Regina gave her a disgusted look. "I've only been here since Ethel checked. That's her name," she started to giggle, "Ethel Gainsford."

"Are you going to come out?" Carrie asked, putting out a hand. "I want to put my clothes away. You can help me if you like."

Regina sprang out, ignoring Carrie's hand. "Why should I? You're supposed to be doing it."

"That's okay. You might miss the present I bought for you, though. It's in with my dresses."

Regina's plain little features—how could she be plain with such good-looking parents—contorted. "Why would you bring a present for me?"

"Why, to make an occasion of our meeting," Carrie said cheerfully. "What else? I'm very pleased to meet you, Regina. I've heard so much about you."

"I bet."

Royce McQuillan hadn't exaggerated when he said his daughter was going on six hundred.

"What did you call me when you first opened the door?" Regina now enquired, looking at Carrie's hair so close to flame.

"I'll try to think…"

"It was Reggie. You called me Reggie."

"I won't if you don't like it."

"I *do*." Regina dressed in a simple T-shirt and shorts suddenly jumped into the armchair. "You must have known I wished I was a boy."

Carrie was upset by that. "What would you want to be a boy for?" She started to hang up her clothes.

"Royce would have liked it," the child said, getting up and absentmindedly handing Carrie another garment. "Royce wants a son."

"Okay, he wants a son." Carrie turned to stare at her. "He wants a daughter, *too*, Reggie. You call your father Royce?" Carrie asked.

"Of course," Regina shrugged her thin shoulders. "He doesn't mind. I think he likes it. I *love* him. He's the best father in the world. You're going to find out sometime, but my mother *hates* me. And that's the truth."

"No, Reggie. Don't think that. Not for a minute," Carrie protested, distressed.

"She's a terrible mother!" said Regina. "She never comes to see me. *Ever*. She never thinks of sending me a present. Where is it, anyway?'' The wrath evaporated into curiosity.

"At the bottom of the suitcase. It's wrapped up.''

"I hope it's not a doll,'' Regina said, sounding like she'd burn it. "I'll swear if it's a doll. I know a good few swearwords. I hear the men.''

"It's not a doll, Reggie,'' Carrie assured her instantly. "There are lots of words you can use besides swearwords, you know.''

"Oh, sure, and I could use them if I wanted to. I can *read*.''

"I'm sure you can,'' Carrie said in a matter-of-fact voice. "Do you like the Harry Potter stories?''

Regina was busy making a mess of Carrie's careful packing. "If I could ever get anyone to buy me one,'' she growled.

"Well, you're in luck.'' Carrie sat down on the bed. "I brought some with me. We can read them together.''

Regina looked at her in astonishment. "Why are you being so sweet to me?''

"Let's say friendly.'' Carrie smiled into the big grey eyes. "I want us to be friends, Reggie. I want that very much.''

For a moment the child looked pleased: small, soft and vulnerable. Then she nodded darkly. "You're just after Royce. They all are. Lindsey says there's not a woman alive who wouldn't want to grab him.''

"You're kidding. She told you that?''

"No one *tells* me anything.'' Regina dug deeper. "But I find ways to hear. Lindsey doesn't like me, either. She told Royce I sneaked your fax.''

"Did you?'' Carrie asked simply.

"No, I didn't.'' Regina stared her in the eyes. "I don't tell lies. *Not one time*.''

"So I believe you.'' Carrie shrugged.

"Those other governesses, they were *wicked!*" Regina told her with some relish.

"That's hard to believe, Reggie," Carrie protested.

"You didn't see the way they acted. Both of them were madly in love with Royce. And there's more." She leaned close to Carrie, her whole body confiding. "Lindsey is in love with him, too." So said, the child began to bounce up and down.

"Reggie, you can't say things like that," Carrie told her.

"I *didn't* say it, Ina did," Regina corrected her, the gymnastics over. "You don't know my aunty Ina. Boy, can she talk! They must think I don't have ears."

Or they didn't care what they said in front of the child. "Here, let me find the present for you," Carrie offered by way of diverting the child's attention. Regina had been rifling through the suitcase, upending everything in the process, now Carrie found the package and handed it to the child.

"What is it?" Regina looked down, somewhat overcome.

"I won't tell you. It's a surprise."

Regina spoke up. "Listen, I'm not going to tell anyone else, but I like you. You're beautiful. I just hope you don't fall in love with Royce."

That brought Carrie up sharply. "Reggie, I'm here to be your friend," she said, ruthlessly suppressing all thought of the child's father.

"So how come you're a governess?" Regina asked. "The other two didn't care about me." While she spoke Regina was making short work of opening the thoughtfully wrapped present, her expression puzzled as she looked down at a gold-lacquered toy trunk. "I can't even guess," she said softly, then opened the lid.

Immediately a clown with a brightly painted face dressed in a polka-dotted nightshirt with a matching bed cap on its head sprang up, waving its arms and turning its head from side to side. It startled the child, making her laugh.

"Isn't that cute!" The big round eyes were filled with radiant pleasure. "The trunk is the bed. Didn't they make a great job of his costume and the bedclothes?" She smoothed them with a finger.

"I'm glad you like it, Reggie." Carrie was really pleased. She'd spent a lot of time choosing the little clown.

"It's cool." Regina looked so soothed Carrie risked asking, "Don't you think we'd better tell Mrs. Gainsford you're found?"

Regina began waving her arms, perfectly mimicking the clown. "Do we have to?"

"Everyone is worried, that's the problem."

Regina waved that possibility away. "I've hidden lots of times before. They don't come looking like they used to."

"As much as you want them to?" Carrie asked, thinking it was Regina's way of getting attention. "You wanted to be found today."

"Yes, I did," Regina confessed, polishing the little clown's red nose. "You wouldn't have found me otherwise. I *wanted* to meet you. Royce said you reminded him of the girl in the painting downstairs. It's supposed to be haunted." She giggled nervously.

"So what does it do?" Carrie asked, "make weird noises or spin upside down in the frame?"

Regina giggled appreciatively. "I don't know *precisely*... But Lindsey told me it was haunted when I went to touch it."

"You do see she was trying to get you *not* to touch it? The painting isn't haunted, Reggie. It's probably very valuable."

"When I told Royce he said, 'you never can tell,' then he laughed."

They were both sitting on the bed playing with the clown when Regina leaned right over speaking in a loud stage whisper. "Don't look now, but Lindsey is behind you."

"She is *not*." Carrie didn't bother to turn her head.

"She is so."

Carrie was just beginning to wonder if the child was serious when Lindsey McQuillan spoke, her voice as sharp as the crack of a whip.

"This won't do at all!" She threw Carrie, who had sprung up off the bed, a look of such severity it would have shaken most governesses to the core.

Carrie, however, turned to face the older woman full-on. "I'm so sorry, Mrs. McQuillan, Reggie and I were on our way downstairs."

Multiple expressions played across Lindsey McQuillan's hard, good-looking face. "Reggie? Is that supposed to be a nickname? The family won't be comfortable with that. Personally I detest the habit of shortening names."

"Well, *I* don't," Regina said flatly, coming to plant herself beside Carrie. "It's my name and *I* like it. Anyway, Royce calls you Lyn. Isn't that the same?"

"That's enough from you, young lady," Lindsey cautioned, visibly angered by the child's rudeness. "You've had the entire household including your father concerned about your whereabouts while you and your new governess—" she shot Carrie another venomous glance "—are calmly sitting up here playing with a toy."

"It was only a few moments, Mrs. McQuillan," Carrie protested.

"It's totally irresponsible," Lindsey pronounced, looking like she wanted both of them flogged. "If you can't do better than that, my advice to Royce will be to send you packing.''

"You're not the boss around here." Regina suddenly started to jump up and down. "I hate you."

For answer, Lindsey McQuillan looked directly at Carrie and said in disgust, "This child is neurotic. Am I right?''

"Gabble…gabble…gabble…" Still yelling, Regina darted out of the room and along the verandah.

Not caring what the other woman thought, Carrie took off after the child, so fleet of foot she caught her up, grasping her in her arms. "Gotcha!"

The yelling and screaming broke into guffaws. The little girl began a mock battle with Carrie who made her own mock attempt to subdue her. "I want the cops right now!'' Regina cried, laughing hard.

"I *am* the cops," Carrie said.

"Show me your badge. So where is it?''

"Your father's got it. It's with my references.''

Abruptly, Regina abandoned the game. "Bloody Lindsey!'' she swore, causing Carrie to take the little girl's thin shoulders and hold them.

"Reggie, you can't use any old swearword that pops into your head. It's not ladylike. Also, you must show your grandaunt the proper respect.''

"I didn't tell her to shut up, did I?'' Regina asked reasonably. "I didn't like the way she was talking to you. Blaming you for everything.''

"She was worried." Carrie tried to make excuses.

Regina groaned. "No, she wasn't. She's lived here for years. You've just arrived.''

"That's true. So will we go downstairs and try to smooth things over?'' Carrie suggested.

"Not me." Regina shook her tangled mop of light brown curls.

"Fine." Carrie patted the child's arm. "I'll go on my own."

"Okay." Regina cheerfully took Carrie by the hand. "Do you think I could ever get to have a hamburger for lunch?"

For a moment Carrie stared at her. "Why ever not? I like hamburgers."

"That's good. I got kicked out of the kitchen the last time I asked for one. Ethel is supposed to be this great cook yet she won't make me a hamburger. With chips. I *love* chips. I hate vegetables, especially broccoli, and I hate cereal for breakfast and I hate eggs."

"Right! I've got the message." Carrie briefly considered Melissa had been a poor eater as a child. "I don't see why you couldn't mix up a drink for yourself for breakfast. Use the blender. I'm sure Mrs. Gainsford has one. A banana smoothie, or you could use pawpaw or cantaloupe. Put some honey on it. Ginger, if you like. We could experiment. Add a scoop of ice cream. You need fattening up."

"And that's not all! Everyone thinks I'm terribly plain." Regina hung her head.

"Who's everyone?" Carrie appeared to challenge.

"All the family, of course. My mother can't bear the sight of me."

"That's really tough." On the evidence, Carrie couldn't argue. "As you're being frank, I might tell you my stepmother couldn't stand the sight of me."

"Really?" Regina looked up at Carrie to make sure she was telling the truth. "She must be a real bitch."

Carrie nodded, so much in agreement she didn't attempt to modify the language. "I'm telling you this in the strictest confidence of course."

"That's okay. I won't tell anyone." Regina reassured

quickly. "How could anyone not like you when you're so beautiful?"

"How can anyone not like you when you're so bright and clever?" Carrie returned.

"You're lying to me," Regina accused solemnly.

Carrie responded quickly. "I'll never lie to you, Reggie. And you'll never lie to me. Will we shake on that?"

Very intensely Regina put out a hand. "Let's," she said.

And that was how Royce McQuillan found them as he reached the upper verandah, Lyn and Mrs. Gainsford in tow. Just like a lynching party, he thought in extreme irritation.

They were solemnly shaking hands.

Brilliant! He studied them both with a shock of pleasure. Only minutes before he'd been informed by an outraged Lindsey in concert with Mrs. Gainsford who raced straight from the kitchen eager to join in, that the new governess was far from an immediate success. Not only had she deliberately withheld vital news Regina had been found, she had given the appearance of actively encouraging the child's bad behaviour.

Now to his great relief it seemed the two culprits were quietly going about the business of making friends.

Thank God! He started counting ten in his mind to bring down his own intense annoyance. He hadn't even left for the Four Mile, taking time off to speak to one of the groundsmen about clearing the overgrown sections of the home gardens when Lyn managed to locate him, which she did with depressing efficiency. She was full of her poor opinion of the new governess. Not that he wasn't used to this lack of enthusiasm. She had given the other girls hell.

Evidently Catrina had hit an especially raw nerve. He'd expected it. Catrina Russell wasn't your everyday Outback governess. Lyn would hate her for that alone. Now he was here to play the heavy. He was sick to death of it. Sick of the constant demands on his time. Sick of Lyn's over-bearing pretentious manner with the household staff. Including the dreary but otherwise excellent Mrs. Gainsford.

Now he greeted Regina with an affectionate smile of relief and Carrie with a calming look. "Hi, poppet. So you decided to turn up?"

"I'd had enough," Regina announced joyfully, puffing out her thin little chest. "I was in the armoire. I frightened Carrie. Now I'm sorry." She ran to her father, clutching him around the knees, such a look of adoration on her small freckled face it gave the tender-hearted Carrie a hard time.

Lift her, she willed Royce McQuillan silently. Lift her. Go on, you're a big strong man. She'd be a little feather in your arms. This is *your daughter*. Kiss her. Hug her. Do something. Don't just stand there, tousling her already over-tousled hair. Disappointment and acute censure stabbed her when he failed to do so, although he continued to smile warmly into the plain little face.

There was not a trace of him in the child, Carrie thought. Not in colouring. Not in feature. Not in potential for height. No trace of her glamorous mother, either, for that matter. Reggie hadn't been fortunate enough to inherit her father's brilliant black eyes, or her mother's ice-blue. They were grey. And I'm going to do something about her hair, Carrie vowed. It could be a big plus for Reggie if it was well cut and properly groomed.

Royce McQuillan catching her naked glance read her thoughts with great accuracy. Obviously she thought him a poor father. Undoubtedly he was. But hell, he wasn't the father and he was doing his best. God only knew who Regina's real father was. One of Sharon's one-night stands when she was drunk. He'd tried to control his bitterness toward Sharon's parents over the years. They had kept

Sharon's instability, which at times became manic, one *huge* secret, though he had to concede childbirth had exacerbated the predisposition.

McQuillan found he didn't much like the look of censure in Catrina's golden eyes. Who was she to judge him? He and Gran were the only ones including Regina's maternal grandparents and her aunt Ina, who actually cared about the child. He hadn't even confided in Gran that Regina wasn't his, though he suspected she had her doubts. The blow had gone too deep. He had fallen out of love with Sharon very quickly but he had been prepared to honour his marriage.

Until she told him with vicious triumph Regina wasn't his.

Now this young woman with an angel's bright aura was judging him and finding him badly wanting. It hurt and he had to admit it made him angry. It was a blow to his self-esteem when he was long accustomed to respect.

Royce was returned to the present by Regina pulling strongly on his hand. "Carrie calls me Reggie. What do you think about that?"

"Reggie's a boy's name," he teased.

"You *want* me to be a boy, don't you?" Regina countered sadly.

"The heck I do!" Now he lifted her, swinging her around and around so she squealed. "Don't *ever* feel I'm not happy with you just the way you are, Reggie. Between the three of us—" he glanced rather coolly in Carrie's direction "—I think it suits you. A bit of fun. One thing, young lady, you have to put on weight."

Reggie hugged him, whispering over his handsome face conspiratorially. "Carrie says I can make my own breakfast. Banana smoothies with ice cream."

"And that's all?" he queried, not thinking it enough.

"A glass of milk," Carrie intervened at this point. "Reggie tells me she doesn't like cereal. Or eggs."

"I can't have a child in my kitchen," Mrs. Gainsford protested, looking quite miffed. "Regina might well have an accident. I don't know what Miss Russell is thinking about."

"Obviously trying to ingratiate herself," Lindsey McQuillan supplied lazily. "I presume you're talking about using a blender?" She shot Carrie a challenging glance. "Regina's too young to be fooling around with appliances. I would have thought you'd know that."

"Well, for a start, I'd be with her," Carrie said, thinking Lindsey McQuillan, striking though she was in appearance, was an awful woman. "There'll be no problem."

"I'd rather they don't do this, Mr. McQuillan," Mrs. Gainsford said reedily, unable to keep her feelings of territorial invasion bottled up.

But Royce McQuillan turned on her smoothly. "As far as I'm concerned, Mrs. Gainsford, we'll employ any method that works. Reggie can have a baked chocolate soufflé fresh out of the oven for breakfast if it will make her *eat*."

"Can I really?" Reggie was delighted, grinning broadly and showing quite a gap between her two front teeth.

"Well, we won't make it routine," he told her. "Now and again."

"You're kiddin' me." She gave him her sunniest smile.

"Miss Russell is the boss," he said suavely.

"No, listen." Reggie shook his hand. "Her name is Carrie. Carrie for Catrina. Isn't that beautiful?"

Royce McQuillan looked at Carrie over the child's head. "I know this new idea won't give Mrs. Gainsford any problems."

"I'm sure we'll be able to manage nicely." Carrie spoke

confidently, aware of his edgy mood toward her. "I expect the kitchen is very large."

Lindsey McQuillan's electric-blue eyes were shooting darts. "Don't think I don't know what you're trying to do," she told Carrie. "But good luck, anyway. I don't plan to be around when Regina sends things crashing to the floor."

That set the complacent child off again. "You're always nasty to me. *Always*." Reggie suddenly screeched in a lightning mood swing, "Bitch. Bitch. Bitch."

"Lovely!" Lindsey mocked while Carrie got her hands beneath the child's armpits and hauled her away saying, "No one has shown me over the house. I'll soon find myself lost if you don't help me, Reggie."

Wiggling, Reggie quickly broke Carrie's restraining grasp but she was calmer now. "It's a pretty good house," she said, taking Carrie's hand. "I won't promise I'll tell you all my hiding places, but I'll tell you some."

"That's okay." Carrie looked down at her, greatly relieved the little girl had settled down. "You won't want to hide with all the good things I've got lined up."

"Tell you what, why don't we start with downstairs?" Reggie swung her head. "Is it okay, Royce, if I show Carrie your study?"

"As long as you promise you won't touch anything," he called, at that moment prepared to forgive Miss Catrina Russell anything for her easy ability to handle this child. He'd never seen Regina, now to be known as Reggie, show this much friendliness to anyone outside himself.

With his plans so disrupted he decided to call in on his grandmother again, walking down the long gallery to the west wing. His grandmother was into her eighties now, her once vibrant health a thing of the past. In fact it was starting to grieve him she just might slip from his life altogether, while he was somewhere out on the station or away on a business trip. Almost time to get in a nurse, though his grandmother would fight him on that one. Jada suited her. Softly spoken, sweet-natured, dignified Jada, she *knew*. But soon the role of minder would be too much even for Jada.

As it was he found the two of them together, talking quietly, companionably, their long thirty-year friendship golden. His grandmother fragile as porcelain but fully dressed in what she called her "uniform," stylish loose shirts over comfortable trousers, lay on her daybed near the French doors, Jada close by in an armchair, a cooling breeze blowing in from the garden, filmy curtains swaying gently. Both looked toward him with smiling surprised faces, Jada, plump with delicate almost birdlike arms and legs, rising out of her chair immediately. "I thought you'd be long gone, Mr. Royce."

"Hell no!" he joked. "Didn't you hear the ruckus?"

"You know we don't hear anything up here, darling." His grandmother tilted her head, her hair beautifully arranged by Jada in a thick French pleat. Another common point between the two women, both had copious snow white hair though Jada wore hers standing up in all directions.

"I thought you two used telepathy?"

Jada chuckled. "Don't need telepathy to guess it was young Regina. She's just gotta be the centre of attention."

"Right on." He saluted her.

"Don't run away too far, Jada," Louise McQuillan called as the aboriginal woman moved to the door. There was something so immensely benign in Jada's spirit just having her around helped ease Louise's pain.

"I'll be right outside the minute Mr. Royce comes down," Jada promised.

"Thank you, dear." Louise McQuillan sighed gratefully. "So tell me, what happened?" With Jada gone she turned her attention to her grandson, fixing him with attentive eyes.

Royce took Jada's unoccupied chair, running the events of the morning before her, making a good story in the process.

His grandmother listened in silence until he'd finished, then she sighed deeply. "I hope Lindsey isn't going to try to make it a trial for this young woman the way she did with the others?"

After what he'd just seen, that amused him. "I think she'll find Catrina quite a different proposition. Catrina grew up holding her own against a stepmother who was no mother at all to her. As for Lindsey…" He shrugged, leaning back into the chair. "I think I'll have to stop her altogether." He'd been thinking that for some time, but Louise McQuillan looked anxious.

"In what way? What do you mean, darling?"

"I'd rather she was out of the house," he answered bluntly, realising his grandmother wasn't fully aware of Lyn's pathetic attempts to fascinate him.

There was an answering sentiment in his grandmother's eyes but an overriding love and pity for her son. "But what about Cameron?" she asked. "He needs us, Royce."

Royce didn't answer, looking down at his hands. No use worrying his grandmother with his scarcely mentionable concerns about his uncle's wife.

"I don't know what demon possessed my poor Cameron to marry her!" Louise McQuillan moaned. "She only married him for money, for so-called position… Even Cameron must be aware of it."

"Of course he is." Royce grimaced in embarrassment. "I think it took him roughly as long to wake up to Lyn as it did for me to wake up to Sharon. Nothing like marriage to help things turn nasty," he added cynically. "I've been thinking very hard of letting Cam take over River Rock.'' He named a distant station in the McQuillan chain.

Louise looked past him to the dancing sheer curtains. ''God forgive me for saying this, my darling, but are you sure Cam could handle it? Both of us love him but both of us know Cameron switched off his engine a long time ago.''

''Doesn't mean he can't rev it up again,'' Royce said a little too crisply, but he was being sorely provoked. ''Cam gets through life just doing what I tell him. It's not the way for a man to go.''

''He hasn't got *your* toughness, my darling,'' Louise pointed out, wryly knowing her grandson didn't even realise just how strong he was. ''Cam never even got a chance to step out of his father's shadow. Trish was the woman who would have been the making of him, but losing Trish the way he did…!'' Louise moved her hands in a desperate little gesture of utter helplessness. Twenty years ago, but she remembered the terrible day of her daughter-in-law's riding accident as though it were yesterday.

''I wonder why it is the good ones are taken?'' Royce asked without ever expecting any answers. ''Unfortunately Cam is married to Lindsey now and she's as good as useless to him. In bed, obviously as they've moved to separate rooms, and as a helpmate. She alienates all the staff. I'm the last person to recommend divorce but I think Cam should cut his losses. God knows I had to.''

Louise nodded sadly. ''To think there was a time I was fond of Sharon,'' she wondered aloud. ''But then, those were the days Sharon and her family were very eager to impress us. It was all such a dreadful, dreadful pretence.''

''You mustn't think about it, Gran,'' he told her briskly. ''Don't add to the stress.''

Louise McQuillan turned her head a little fretfully. ''I know I *shouldn't*, but these days I have too much time to think. Too much time to go over our tragedies. But don't worry, my darling." She suddenly bucked up. "I'm not going to die until I see you happily remarried to the right woman. I've struck a bargain with the Almighty."

"Great!" He gave her his beautiful heart-melting smile and stood up. "If anyone has the clout, it's you. You could be my only salvation, Gran." He bent to kiss her.

"No!" She patted the strong hand that was resting on the head of her daybed. "There will be the woman for you. I can feel her coming closer. The answer to my prayers."

He had reached her bedroom door before she called after him rather coquettishly. "Your Catrina sounds a very interesting young woman."

"*My* Catrina, Gran?" His brilliant black eyes mocked her.

"Odd the way our first McQuillan bride was Catriona," Louise mused. "That rare amber colouring, as well."

He gave a little hoot of laughter. "Don't start seeing omens, Gran. Our new governess was a student up until a year ago. She's very *young* and she has a trauma to overcome."

"Does she know I was a fine pianist in my day?" Louise McQuillan asked.

"Haven't said a thing. It didn't seem the subject to get on to."

"She won't fail to notice the concert grand. Even if Mrs. Gainsford keeps covering it up."

"Gainsford means well, Gran," he told her. "No one has played the piano for years. The cover keeps the dust out."

His grandmother smiled and waved him off. "But pianos are meant to be played, my darling. Your Catrina might very well come to it in her own time."

CHAPTER SIX

THE lights were on in this huge house. Carrie walked down the left side of the divided staircase that made such a striking approach to the principal rooms dazzled by the astonishing brilliance of Maramba homestead at night. Everything was light and glitter. Recessed spotlights flared over the wonderful collection of objects evoking the South East Asian heritage, the tall eight-panel Coromandel screens inlaid with jade and ivory and semiprecious stones, the rugs and sculptures, the tall Chinese vases, including the big matching fish bowls on carved stands that flanked the staircase at ground level.

Someone in the last hour or so had filled the bowls to overflowing with golden-yellow cymbidiums. She caught her breath at their beauty, pausing to admire them. The bright yellow was in wonderful contrast to the inky blue-and-white pattern of the large porcelain bowls.

She knew from her tour with Reggie, the magnificent living room was to her right. It housed not only the "haunted" portrait of a ravishingly pretty young girl in a sunlit garden setting who just happened to have Carrie's own unusual colouring, but a nine-foot concert grand someone had swathed in a gorgeous bolt of brocade. Seeing the piano had given her an actual frisson of shock as though what she sought to escape had followed her to this remote place; wasn't the world big enough or wide enough for there not to be a piano? No ordinary piano, either. Although she hadn't approached it and it appeared to mean nothing out of the ordinary to Reggie, it was obvious someone in the family had played the piano at some time. Because of the size and value of the instrument, she concluded that someone had played it extremely well. Yet Royce McQuillan had never said a word.

Carrie continued on, passing through the library that contained an extensive collection of books to the formal dining room beyond. This was a huge room used for large gatherings, beyond that was the informal dining room used by the family. She understood that was where they would be dining tonight. Voices reached her as she approached the lovely luxuriant plant-filled room with its floor-to-ceiling glass walls that allowed a wonderful view over the lush tropical grounds.

Inside, seated at ease in chairs, was the family who all turned to look at her. Royce McQuillan—stunning enough to set *any* woman's heart racing, she excused her own reaction—who immediately stood up and walked toward her; and a frail little lady with the sweetest face and expression, dressed in elegant silver evening pyjamas. Mrs. Louise McQuillan, it had to be, Carrie guessed. A tall, gently distinguished-looking man rather like a university professor but enough like Royce McQuillan to be his uncle, now also stood and, her face turned in a practiced silky smile, the glamorous Lindsey in a floral print halter dress that showed a bit too much cleavage for a family dinner.

"You timed that nicely," Royce McQuillan told Carrie when he reached her, taking her lightly by the arm. "How lovely you look," he added quite without thinking. She did indeed look lovely. "We were just having a predinner drink. Come meet the rest of the family."

She was content to let him steer her, feeling his dangerous power as his hand closed over her bare arm. She stood first in front of his grandmother who greeted her with unconcealed pleasure and interest, right hand up-stretched.

"I want you to be happy here, my dear." Louise McQuillan smiled. Her smile was beautiful just like her grandson's, and there was a real light in her still fine dark eyes.

"I adore it already, Mrs. McQuillan," Carrie answered with happy emphasis. She had taken to Mrs. McQuillan senior on sight, thinking she must have been very beautiful when she was young. As they spoke Carrie found herself gently stoking rather than shaking the hand offered her for fear of crushing it. The fingers were so fragile, even though the joints were knotted and swollen. Long fingers that once must have been as strong as her own. It was an oddly intimate moment that passed between young and old but neither woman seemed to find it strange.

Royce McQuillan's uncle Cam in turn took Carrie's hand as gently as she had taken his mother's, his manner almost "old worldly" courteous. He was one of those men usually defined as a "perfect gentleman," handsome, erect, his manner graceful, but he had none of the vibrant energy, that aura of power that made his nephew so out-standing. Rather he seemed like a man not really *involved.* Not the quintessential cattleman.

When she reached Lindsey, Carrie was offered a rather flippant "hello there," but Lindsey's electric-blue eyes moved over Carrie's outfit like a monitoring device, totting up each individual item. Carrie had chosen a dress that suited her well, a deceptively simple peach silk shift but with a very clever bias cut. Strappy sandals were on her feet. Sale price Ferrangamo and even then they had been dear enough.

"Don't tell me you managed to get Regina to bed?" Lindsey finally asked, apparently not happy about the final figure.

"No struggle at all." Carrie smiled. "The two of us started on one of the children's stories I brought with me. Eventually Reggie nodded off."

"Reggie only needs the right handling," Louise

McQuillan said gently, picking up on the new nickname and looking at Carrie with open approval. "I've been saying that for quite a while."

"Early days, Gran," Lindsey warned, her strong features sceptical.

It was over dinner Carrie was treated to one of the reasons the less than mellow Mrs. Gainsford had managed to keep her job. She was a great cook. In fact Carrie thought Mrs. Gainsford could teach Melissa a lot. Carrie didn't know how Mrs. Gainsford did it—surely most great cooks had a little bit of the show-off in them?—but dinner was superb. It took Carrie a little while to realise only she and Royce McQuillan were actually doing justice to such a beautifully cooked and presented meal. Louise McQuillan ate very very sparingly, tiny mouthfuls of the great North Queensland eating fish, the barramundi, served with a crab cream sauce on a little white vegetable mash. Lindsey delicately forked over her seared scallops; while Cameron McQuillan seemed to be lost in some monumental problem he couldn't tell them all about. He appeared to come out of his reverie briefly to say he might try a slice of orange and Grand Marnier soufflé cake with coffee. No mascarpone, thank you.

The conversation was general but when Carrie expressed her fascination with the broad landscape and the wonderful sense of "belonging" with both the homestead and the home gardens, Louise McQuillan came to full life. She turned to Carrie with a flush of pleasure. "My first job as a bride was to make a great tropical park out of what were then *wild* surroundings. It was an immense challenge. I was only twenty yet my husband gave me complete control and an army of helpers. One day when I'm feeling stronger I'll show you what I had done all those years ago, Catrina, as you're interested."

"Indeed I am. I'd enjoy that very much, Mrs. McQuillan."

"It was Royce's idea to construct the waterfall at the narrow end of the lagoon," she said, looking down the dark polished table to her grandson.

"A real brainwave." Royce smiled, his glance resting on Carrie, who looked as colourful and shiny as a day lily. "I had boulders brought in from all over the station. God knows how the great landscape gardeners of centuries past managed without modern machinery to perform the Herculean tasks. I used bulldozers, backhoes, excavators, even the station helicopter. While we were at it we contoured the surrounds of the lagoon to make it even more attractive. Roughly five thousand litres of water a minute pass over the waterfall when the valve is fully open. The water supply comes from the dam behind the homestead. I'll show you when I have the time."

"I'd love to see the waterfall in operation," Carrie said, not sure of the exact nature of her feelings toward Royce McQuillan, but they were powerful.

"You will," he promised lazily. "Gran and I decided on a tree fern forest at that end, then with so much water about she hit on the idea of stepped terraces of water iris. There are millions of them, as you'll see. Great beds of day lilies and arum lilies, too. My mother and Gran spent endless hours working out different themes for the grounds."

"Rosemary and I were such friends!" Louise McQuillan shook her head sadly. "The home gardens were our passion. If you want to see truly wonderful fruit and vegetable gardens then you'll have to find your way to the rear of the house near the old stables. That's where Rosemary truly reigned supreme. It was absolutely thrilling picking all the fruits and vegetables she had grown.

The extraordinary thing was neither of us had any great expertise when we started. Just a great love of gardens.''

''I couldn't bear to break my fingernails,'' Lindsey McQuillan volunteered languidly. ''My pleasure is looking at the gardens, not breaking my back. Whilst we're on the subject of gardens, I do hope you told Carrie about the snakes, Royce? That may very well bother her.''

Louise McQuillan opened wide her eyes. ''I've lived here for sixty years, without incident, Lindsey. Snakes do their best to keep out of the way. I can't think Catrina would ever be foolish enough to try to pick one up?''

''I'll leave the snake charming to those who can handle it.'' Catrina laughed. ''Snakes or not, I'm enchanted with everything.''

It wasn't until they adjourned to the seating area for coffee that the general conversation turned to the specific as Lindsey decided to show her talent for investigation.

''A little bird tells me you play the piano, Carrie,'' she announced brightly, glancing closely at Carrie to see how she was taking this disclosure. ''You'll have easy access to one here. That's if Gran will allow you to play her Steinway?''

Carrie felt too shocked to be angry though the speed with which her confidence had been breached filled her with the sick realisation. Royce McQuillan must have told this malicious woman all about her. Either Royce McQuillan or his grandmother. Whoever it was Carrie felt a jolt of betrayal.

It must have showed.

''Oh, I'm sorry. How awful. You had an accident didn't you?'' Lindsey cried as though she only just recalled that piece of information.

That appeared to arouse Royce's disgust. ''And how did you stumble on this?'' he interjected before Lindsey could continue, not bothering to dissipate the hostility in his dark vibrant voice. "Don't tell us." He laughed without humour. "Sharon, through her willing stooge, Ina?"

"But, Royce, I thought you liked Ina?" Lindsey eyed him mock quizzically. "I told you this morning I had a conversation with her. But you didn't want to know about it."

The knowledge Royce McQuillan hadn't confided in Lindsey did much to restore Carrie's composure. "What I don't understand is why either Mrs. Sharon McQuillan or her sister would be interested in me?" she queried.

Lindsey laughed, a flash of white teeth between very red lips. "That's simple, really. Sharon continues to be interested in any woman who comes into this house. You appear to have gone a little pale, Carrie. I do hope I haven't upset you?"

Carrie was quiet for a moment, considering. "You've surprised me, that's all. I was hoping to forget my accident for a while."

Lindsey nodded sympathetically. "I can understand that, but surely it won't go away?"

"Lindsey, please!" Louise McQuillan looked distressed. "I do wish you would change the subject," she requested. "Catrina is handling her own problems in her own way. I might mention here and now, Catrina," she turned her small face to Carrie, "you're more than welcome to go to the piano whenever you feel you can."

Carrie smiled at the old lady gratefully. "Thank you, Mrs. McQuillan. It's not easy at the moment, as you can imagine."

"No, my dear," Louise soothed. "But I know you will find courage."

At the sympathy and liking in the old lady's voice, Lindsey's jealousy cracked open. "Surely it isn't that much of a tragedy?" she asked. "You can lead a full life."

She looked at Carrie challengingly. "It's not as though you've lost a limb."

Suddenly her stepmother's face came back to her. This was the sort of thing Glenda said. "I really don't think you'd know much about it, Mrs. McQuillan," Carrie answered quietly. "I've been very involved in my music all my life. I love it. I've trained for it. I could have had a career."

"Then it's decidedly odd you accepted the post of governess," Lindsey retaliated. "Whoever suggested it?" Her bright blue glance whipped from Carrie to Royce.

"Don't bother asking," Royce said. "It's none of your business, Lyn."

"That's perfectly true." Cameron McQuillan had taken overlong to curb his wife. "It might be best, too, if you don't give Ina the slightest encouragement to gossip, Lyn. Sharon is not part of the family anymore."

"Someone should tell *her*." Lindsey flushed at her husband's mild reprimand. "It wasn't as though I was asking for information about Miss Russell. It was volunteered. Personally I can't see why the secrecy."

"I wasn't aware Catrina kept any secret from *me*," Royce drawled. He looked at Lindsey, his black eyes sardonic. "Catrina has to deal with the loss of a promising career. If she doesn't want to talk about it, that's her affair. When you're talking to Ina next you might break some news to her. She won't be on the guest list this Christmas."

"How drastic!" Lindsey sneered before she could help herself. "She lives for these visits. Like Sharon, she'll never get you out of her system."

"As though I care about such things," Royce told her with slow cruelty. "Gran, this can't be very pleasant for you."

"On the contrary, it's been delightful meeting Catrina."

Louise McQuillan smiled. "I'm hoping, Catrina, you won't leave me to my solitude," she said charmingly. "You must come visit me. We can talk."

"I'd like that, Mrs. McQuillan." There was gratitude in Carrie's golden eyes. She felt touched and honoured the old lady had made the effort to come down to dinner to meet her.

"Now—" Louise McQuillan looked at her grandson once more, her delicate head shaking almost imperceptibly on its fragile neck "—my bed calls. I think you can help me upstairs, my darling."

"Sure, Gran." Immediately Royce stood up, as did Cameron who went to his mother, bent over her and kissed her cheek.

"Goodnight, Mother."

"Goodnight, Cameron, dear." She patted his large, strong hand.

Carrie excused herself after saying she was going for a walk leaving that extraordinarily ill-matched couple, Lindsey and Cameron McQuillan together to perhaps bicker lovingly. They didn't appear to have a thing in common, but far more worrying to Carrie's mind, was the fact Mrs. Lindsey McQuillan appeared far more attracted to her husband's nephew than she ever was to him. A potential mine field? Almost unreal.

It was with a feeling of relief Carrie found her way out to the huge lobby, from there taking the front stairs to the home gardens. It was a beautiful night, the vast landscape lit by a huge copper moon, the languorous golden moon of the tropics. She took the broad gravel path set with irregular-shaped paving stones that meandered around the house, intending to take a short walk before retiring. She had never in her life ventured into a garden of such immense proportions, a million blossoms scenting the night with their presence. Bright moonlight lit her way burnishing the shining, still waters of the lagoon. She was tempted to walk down to the water, it looked so inviting but decided until she knew more about her surroundings it would be better to stick literally to the garden path.

It perturbed her Royce's wife had gone to such lengths to check out her background. And so quickly. She must have spies everywhere. It hadn't helped Ina's cause, either, getting straight onto Lindsey to relay the findings. Three women all obsessing about the same man. Royce McQuillan very obviously was one of those men women found irresistible. It wasn't just his handsomeness though "handsome" didn't say it, it was his whole aura. She felt like she was unravelling more and more herself. Even her accident didn't seem to matter as much as it had. Carrie pressed her injured finger, the little finger, against her warm cheek. She was far away from everyone she loved, her father, Melissa, Jamie and Liz. Far away from her friends. She could see how it was going to be with Lindsey McQuillan. No ally there. In fact, an enemy. Feeling the way she did about Royce McQuillan, why was Lindsey staying here? Surely it would be better for her and her husband to set up a home of their own. Their marriage had no chance of survival with Lindsey feeding on forbidden fantasies.

Carrie continued to walk, lost in thought. She didn't think she was going to have that much trouble discharging her duties as governess. Reggie, after an initial shaky start, had turned out to be surprisingly amenable. On their tour of the house she had been an engaging little companion with a knowledge of beautiful objects and far-off places far beyond her years.

To ease the meal hour, Carrie had persuaded Mrs. Gainsford to cook morsels of fish in batter for Reggie's tea served with chips and presented in a little basket lined with a strong paper napkin. Carrie who knew a little bit about napkin art then went to the trouble of making a waterlily for Reggie's plate, later showing the child how she went about folding the napkin over and over before she was able to gently pull the corners upward to make the petals. Reggie had been fascinated, eating her meal with every evidence of enjoyment, something that pleased Mrs. Gainsford so much she went to a drawer, pulled out a large starched napkin and proceeded to fashion it into a bishop's hat, which she set beside the waterlily. Reggie had clapped. Mrs. Gainsford had smiled. Simple little measures but they succeeded in making the mealtime quite pleasant.

Some twenty or so minutes later Carrie, refreshed, her lungs filled with the pure night air, turned to retrace her steps, her eyes delighting in the spectacle of the house lit up like an ocean-going liner at night. This was such an experience for her. A tropical adventure. One she had never even imagined a little more than a week ago. She was finding out things she hadn't even known about herself. Things inside her. Wild stirrings in the blood, the ravishing pleasure of just being able to look at a certain man. To study the planes and angles of his face. The set of his shoulders, the elegance and strength of his body. To listen to his voice. Get caught up in his smile. To sink near to drowning in the sparkle of his eyes. Her own extravagant feelings invested Lindsey McQuillan's barely concealed longings with pathos. Here was a woman who had married a much older man for status then fallen in love with his nephew. What a recipe for disaster.

Carrie was nearing the corner of the east wing outside the library when she saw through the open French doors a sight that froze her with dread. Royce McQuillan in a temper—or some flame of passion—was gripping Lindsey McQuillan by the shoulders, his striking face usually so vivid with life, taut with fury. She was staring up into his face, rapt, stupefied, begging? Her head with its short crop of blond hair flung back, in some turbulence of her own. Whatever words were passing between them, Carrie couldn't catch but the body language was abundantly clear. Both were intensely aroused.

The shock was so extreme Carrie felt as winded as if she'd been struck in the chest. She recoiled in misery, left the path and broke into a run clutching at the heart that had leapt up in her breast. This can't *be!* she cried raggedly, talking out loud like a child. They can't be having an affair. No matter what she saw, what she thought she saw, it couldn't be true. For all he incited strong passions, she couldn't see Royce McQuillan betraying his uncle.

Where there was smoke there was fire, the night answered her.

Carrie's headlong flight took her down the grassy slope to the sanctuary of the lagoon. Her insides were contracting, a taste of bitterness was in her mouth. That grass was so thick and plush the heels of her sandals were sinking into its deep pile. She could smell the water, hear the ghost of music in the vibration of the reeds, see the luminous heads of hundreds of white arum lilies. Inevitably her mind grappled with the thought of snakes. What to do next? Wait until her heartbeat had settled and she had regained her composure before making her way back up the slope onto the path. She didn't know if she had it in her to hum some snatch of melody to warn of her approach. Hadn't Lindsey told him the governess had gone for a walk? Or were both so far gone as not to care?

Bemused, Carrie hovered in the dark shadows at the water's edge, relegated to the role of unwitting voyeur. The things one saw through windows! Enough to shatter lives. Darkness was all around her. She couldn't be visible from the house yet moments later she saw Royce McQuillan's tall figure silhouetted against the brilliant lights from the lobby before he strode out onto the verandah like a man in need of a great breath of fresh air.

He stood for a moment, looking out into the night, then he plunged down the stairs.

Carrie's need to avoid him burned so strong she found herself taking off, running through the grass following the upward contour of the lagoon until she could reach the protection of one of the great shade trees. From there, after a minutes respite, she could make her way to the house, perhaps entering through one of the multiple sets of French doors. Entry by stealth, she thought. My first night and I'm sneaking back into the house.

It's all your fault, Royce McQuillan, she thought, her mind locked into an obsessive replay of what she had seen. Lust? Guilt? Anger? Degrees of all three. Carrie realised she was trembling, her breath coming in little keening sounds through her nostrils. If she fell she could ruck an ankle. This was like some hellish dream.

"For God's sake!" A man's voice astonished her. How had he got there? Yet arms like steel bands locked around her, bringing her flight to a shuddering halt. "If I live to be a hundred I'll never understand why women do the things they do," Royce McQuillan rasped.

She tried to laugh but, couldn't possibly succeed. Instead her breath spasmed. "I'm sorry I became disoriented in the dark."

"Couldn't you have stuck to the path?" He could feel the tremble in her body through her silky taut skin, moonlight pearling down on a face sheened with heat. He recognised the sensation every time he touched her. Tried to disconnect it.

"I wanted to look at the water." She was fighting for breath, for control.

"Listen." He continued to keep hold of her, barely preventing himself from shaking her. "I can't tell you more than one time. Don't go straying from the paths at night. Especially don't go walking around near the water. Some areas are swampy, you could have got locked in reeds. I would have thought you'd have more sense. You haven't even got anything substantial on your feet. Little bits of leather!''

"I forgot. I'm sorry." She stood like a statue within his arms, willing herself to feel nothing. "I won't do it again."

"Hell, girl, it's my responsibility to see you're safe," he said with sharp impatience.

"Look, I'm all right." Carrie felt her energy returning as though she had drawn off some of his virile strength. "I don't need you to walk me back."

He turned her face fully to look at him. "Something has upset you."

"I can deal with it." Her body went very tense.

"*Tell* me."

"I'd rather die first." Hostility flooded her.

"It must be pretty awful. You were out on the path, weren't you?" His voice cracked with a kind of contempt.

"I hope I'm not going to have to account for all of my movements?"

"Ahh, the little flash of hostility. Such a dead give-away."

"I really don't want to talk about it." Indeed she didn't, feeling sealed off in a strange world.

"You don't have to hide anything from me," he jeered. "You saw something—you *thought* you saw something— that made you so uncomfortable you tore off into the night?"

"Why don't we just leave this?" Carrie knew immediately her voice sounded too tense, too judgemental.

"How sanctimonious can you get?" he swore gently. "Leave *what*?"

She dropped her head, her hair falling around her face

like a curtain. "I suppose sometimes only the truth will do."

"And you're sufficiently sure of your facts to know it? Let me spare you the telling, Carrie. You looked into the house and saw Lindsey and me having a few heated words?"

"Something like that," she confessed in a low voice. Even now he hadn't settled down.

"Why should it upset you so badly?" He stared at her. "It's hardly any of your business."

"I don't see it like that. I was very disturbed."

"You thought you'd actually stumbled on an illicit love scene?" he scoffed.

"No need to be so cutting." She felt a wave of shame.

"No need for you to play the shining paragon of virtue, either. So bright and so innocent. For your edification, Miss Russell, I am not, repeat, *not* having an affair with my uncle's wife, if that's the conclusion you jumped to. Did you really think I was? Did you *really* think that of me?"

She shook her head wretchedly. "No, I didn't. I certainly didn't want to. But she's in love with you. You must know that."

"That's what it looked like?" he asked in a harsh, drawn voice.

"That was the message I've got since I arrived."

"Congratulations!" he groaned.

"What did you say to her?" Carrie found herself asking before she could stop herself.

"Just who the hell do you think you are?" he asked in amazement, trying to rein in his own feelings. "You're obviously not happy just being Reggie's governess."

"I'm no more a governess than the hostess of a game show," she said with a spark of anger, not going to stand there and be humiliated. "I didn't pick the place and I didn't pick the time. I just happened to look into a brightly lit room—''

"Be sure to add, and passed judgement on what you saw."

Carrie glanced up at the moon as if for guidance... "So I regret what happened. I regret if I've offended you. I know you'd never betray your uncle."

"Is there anything you'd like to add to that?" he demanded, closing his fingers around her wrist.

"Yes, don't be mad at me. Please."

Abruptly he relented, his thumb almost absently stroking the transparent blue-and-white inside skin. "Okay, a ceasefire. We'll walk for a while, then we'll go back to the house. But first I'd like to tell you the idea of Lindsey's being in love with me is a joke. An embarrassment. There's a whole body of literature about women who put themselves through torture with their ridiculous longings. To put it crudely, Lyn isn't getting the kind of sex she wants and she seems to want it pretty badly that's my interpretation anyway, but she's not getting it from me. We can all be very certain about that. I've made it so plain I expect she's going to devote the rest of her life to hating me."

"Lord!" Carrie ached. "Love is an illness."

"*Not* love."

"It must seem like it. Sexual confusions. Couldn't Lindsey and your uncle live somewhere else? I understand he's very well off."

"A fact that appears to have all but destroyed him," he answered bluntly.

"Your uncle should be enjoying life. He's a charming man."

"And *kind*, which I remind you, I'm not. Cam's too withdrawn if not actually out of it. In many ways he's his own worst enemy."

"That's sad." Carrie's voice wavered. His touch was inducing such excitement.

"Okay, it's sad, but I'm losing patience."

"They're such an unlikely couple." She toyed with the idea of pulling her hand away but didn't.

"Hell, he's not the only man to marry the wrong woman." His voice carried self-disgust. "Cam and I between us have made it a family affair."

She tried to absorb some of his anger. "You'll meet the right woman," she promised.

"What, are you going to set up shop as a clairvoyant now?" he scoffed, glancing down at her silky head, her pure profile outlined against the gilded purple of the night.

"No, I'm just trying to be cheerful."

"How sweet of you." The vibrant voice was attractively discordant.

"Don't be bitter. The smartest people can make terrible mistakes."

To her surprise he gave a hoot of genuine laughter. "Catrina, for one so young your insight is tremendous."

"Insightful. That's me. Dammit!"

"Hey, I like it." Before she knew what he was about, he turned her to him, cupping her oval face in his hands. "What are you doing in my life?"

She had no time to answer even if she could because he bent his head to kiss her parted mouth. Gently...so gently, yet her heart beat like a wild thing, nibbling at her cushioned lips as he might at wild strawberries. It was utterly bewitching, emotive enough to make her want to cry. She could have spent her life kissing him. Yet when he finally withdrew his beautiful seductive mouth from hers she could only find a stammer. "You said you wouldn't k-k...kiss me again," she reminded him.

He nodded. "I meant it, too. At the time." His tone was

both erotic and tender as he pushed the hot silk of her hair behind her ears.

"Well, you shouldn't do it. I can't think straight," Carrie answered.

"That's your punishment," he said crisply. "Never, never, spy on me again. I'm your employer, after all. Which is a kind of shame." He caught her hand and began to swing it, urging her on toward the house.

"Did you have these little problems with my predecessors?" she couldn't resist asking as he hauled her up onto the path.

"They weren't as shatteringly attractive as you are," he mocked. "I just can't believe it! I didn't know you a fortnight ago."

"It is odd," Carrie agreed as he steadied her. More than odd, astonishing! Suddenly after all the many long months of her crushing disappointment the whole world looked different. She raised her face to him as they walked up onto the drive.

"Look at the stars," he said, pausing to rest his hand on her delicate shoulder. "The Southern Cross. Orion the mighty hunter with his jewelled belt. The others like diamond clusters through the trees. No matter what happens to us they never change. They endure."

"As we're supposed to do," she said quietly, feeling the warmth and the energy spreading out from his hand. She had to find a way out of her own confusions. Her long years of training couldn't be lost.

"Sometimes things get worse before they get better, Catrina," he warned as though he had read her mind. "Put up a fight."

"I'm going to."

They lingered for a little while longer, he talking, Carrie listening, perfectly in tune with his mood.

Neither noticed the woman standing in the shadows of the upstairs verandah. Nor did they know how long she had been there.

CHAPTER SEVEN

REGGIE, to everyone's delight, slipped virtually overnight into another skin. She became a pleasant and co-operative child blossoming under Carrie's gentle understanding hand, secure in the knowledge Carrie really liked her, for Carrie's approval and quick affection for this motherless little girl was transparent.

By the end of a month, in the light of what had gone on before, they had established an excellent working routine; three hours of lessons in the morning; two in the afternoon. Again contrary to all Carrie had been told, Reggie proved an apt pupil. The trick Carrie had found from her own teaching experiences with gifted young musicians was to make the subject matter interesting, something she gave much thought to. That done, learning flowed very naturally. Reggie had a large vocabulary for her age—even excluding the swearwords which continued to pop out from time to time—but her disinterest in numeracy took an upward turn when Carrie hit on using an assortment of large, brightly printed cards to help Reggie see problem-solving more as a game.

Meal times, too, were much less of a battleground. Even Mrs. Gainsford had to admit Carrie's methods were working. Reggie learned how to make her own breakfast smoothies—banana remained the favourite—and Mrs. Gainsford capitulated to the extent ''kid's meals'' were on the menu with Reggie making a big concession by eating certain julienned raw vegetables she could dip in a sauce. All this along with many chocolate-flavoured malted milks resulted in a pleasing weight gain. Reggie had never had such a benevolent guiding hand. And it showed!

So it wouldn't be all work and no play, they often drove out for a picnic lunch followed by a nature ramble always within a specified distance of the homestead. Royce McQuillan had put at Carrie's disposal a nifty little Toyota Rav 4 which gave her considerable mobility. In fact she sometimes thought he would give her just about anything if it would make her stay happy and Reggie a contented child.

Reggie adored their little forays into the bush but not for the life of her could Carrie cajole the little girl into learning to swim. There was a beautiful big swimming pool in the rear garden of the homestead but of far more interest and pleasure to Carrie was a wonderful rock pool fed by a fresh water spring some four miles from the main compound. Almost perfectly moon-shaped, it nestled in the shelter of a series of low jutting rocks massed like an amphitheatre, crystal-clear, rather cold even in extreme heat, surrounded by tall spears of blue native grasses overhung at this time of the year by a feathery tree with dazzling yellow, large-petalled flowers.

On this particular day they had finished their picnic lunch. Reggie dressed in a pink T-shirt and shorts, sat on a large flat rock overlooking the pool, watching Carrie taking her swim.

"You look like a mermaid," Reggie called as Carrie floated on her back, her hair streaming around her.

"It's lovely in here." Carrie would have loved to induce the child to enter the water. But all in her own good time.

"No way!" Reggie shook her head. "There are spirits at the bottom of the pools."

"Spirits?" For a moment Carrie thought she hadn't heard right. She swam over to the child, treading water. "Did you say spirits?"

"They'll get you, too," Reggie warned.

Carrie shook her head. "This is a beautiful place, Reggie. Can't you feel peace and harmony all around you?"

"Yes, I can," Reggie answered simply, "but there are all spooky things, too."

"Who said?" Carrie pulled herself out of the pool, water streaming from her slender long-legged body, clad in a streamlined dark blue swimsuit with a splash of green and yellow flowers.

Reggie ran to pick up Carrie's towel, passing it to her and gazing up at Carrie with open admiration. "You've got a beaut figure."

Carrie could feel herself smiling. "Why, thank you, Reggie. I'm getting a lot of exercise these days."

"Uncle Cam told Royce you're the most beautiful girl he's ever seen. And you know what? He said it in front of Lindsey."

"Ouch!" Carrie rubbed herself down briskly, thinking Lindsey wouldn't have liked that.

"Uncle Cam just says what he thinks." Reggie smiled. "He's a nice man, isn't he? But so *quiet.*"

"He's a perfect sweetie," Carrie said honestly. She had got to know Cameron McQuillan better. "I think his quietness is the result of a lot of unresolved sadness, Reggie."

Reggie, justly proud of her word comprehension was lost. "I just forgot what that means?"

"Unresolved?" Carrie asked.

Reggie nodded.

"It means sadness not properly dealt with. When your uncle Cam lost his first wife the grief was so terrible he couldn't ever break it down into little pieces. Something he could manage. It has never gone away. Some people are like that." Carrie thought of her own father and the unresolved grief over her mother he had expressed. "Men can feel things very deeply."

Reggie nodded in near adult agreement. "So why did he marry Lyn then?" she asked reasonably.

"He must have thought she'd bring joy back into his life." Carrie towelled her hair. "She's a striking-looking woman."

"That's not her own blond hair," Reggie said. "Haven't you seen the roots?"

"Lots of women colour their hair, Reggie. It looks good."

"She doesn't frighten me anymore," Reggie said, pitching a small pebble across the water.

"I should hope not," Carrie breathed, very protective of the child.

"She *did.* She even told Ina she never thought I was one of them."

"One of what?" Carrie looked at her in dismay.

"I dunno. I think she's mad. Anyway she's the one who told me about the spirits at the bottom of the lagoon at home. Evil little things that will catch you around the ankles and drag you down to the bottom. She knows I can't swim. I would drown."

Carrie made a note to speak to Lindsey. "I could teach you to swim in no time, Reggie, if you'll let me." Carrie put certainty and commitment into her voice. "You could never be frightened with me?"

"Don't be silly! You're neat! I'll think about it, Carrie," Reggie promised. "But not today."

"That's okay." Carrie was satisfied with that much progress. She ran a wide-toothed comb through her wet hair then pulled it back into a ponytail. "I suppose we should think about starting back," she said regretfully.

"Don't you want to dry off?" Reggie was happy where she was.

"I'd like to." Carrie weakened.

"I love it here." Reggie sighed in contentment as Carrie spread her towel on a rock then lay down in the shade of the overhanging tree, with diamond chunks of sunlight falling on her long legs. After a while Reggie spoke. "You know we've got crocs on Maramba?"

Carrie's breath literally whistled. "Wh-a-a-t!" She pulled up her long legs so swiftly a great armoured reptile might have lunged out of the water beneath her.

"Not here, silly." Reggie giggled. "This is freshwater. So are the billabongs. I'm talking about upcountry. Royce might take us. Up near the estuary where the salties, that's the salt water crocodiles, come in. Not so many as there used to be. You don't think Royce would let us swim anywhere there was a salt water croc?"

"Hang on, I'm feeling a little weak," Carrie begged, still startled. "No, of course not. You gave me a start."

"I'm so sorry!" Reggie sweetly apologised. "I didn't mean to. I was hoping you'd ask Royce to take us up-country. We could go in the helicopter."

"I don't know I'm all that interested in meeting your rough-skinned pals," Carrie said wryly.

"They're fascinating!" Reggie breathed. "The first time I saw one out of the water I thought it was a great big log."

"Some log!" Carrie shuddered, turning her head at some disturbance behind them.

A lone rider was coming down the trail, calling out to them as he approached. "Want some company?"

"Nah, you're supposed to be working," Reggie called back, laughing. "I'll tell Royce."

"Gimme a break, princess." The rider dismounted, hitching his horse's reins to a branch. He was young, lanky, whip-cord thin, attractive with straw-coloured curls and bright hazel eyes. His name was Tim Barton. He was the son of a wealthy Melbourne merchant banker, a long-time friend of the McQuillan family, and he was doing a year's work experience on Maramba as a jackeroo. A kind of toughening-up process before he joined the family firm, Carrie gathered. She had met Tim several times on her trips around the station and quite liked him though it was obvious Tim wasn't taking his duties as seriously as he might have done. On his own admission he wanted to exact every bit of colour and fun he could out of his stay. Carrie he had taken to at first glance.

Now he ambled down the grassy slope, swaggering a little in his riding boots, cream Akubra in hand.

"How are you, Carrie?" He stared at her with open admiration, eagerly soaking her in.

"Fine, Tim." She gave him an uncomplicated smile. "Doesn't this come under the category of wasting time?"

He laughed good-naturedly. "Never wasting time talking to a pretty girl. *Girls.*" He bowed in Reggie's direction.

Reggie shook her curly mop. "You're here to see Carrie. Royce said you fancy yourself as a lady's man."

Tim's ears reddened. "You're something, you are, Reggie. Carrie taught you to swim yet?"

"The water's not warm enough," Reggie explained. "Like an apple?"

"No way I'm going to take it off you."

"That's okay." Reggie threw a shiny red apply his way. "What do you want, anyway?"

Tim glanced at Carrie, a wry expression in his eyes. "I swear this kid's a grown woman. Actually I wanted to ask Carrie if she'd like to go riding at the weekend. I know plenty of great trails. I have Saturday afternoon off."

"Sure, we'd love to come," Reggie answered promptly for both of them.

"I don't know that I asked you, princess," Tim said mildly. "Anyway, you're too little to ride."

"I am not! Don't say that," Reggie answered indignantly. "I haven't been ready for it, but I am now. Carrie is going to teach me."

"Seems to me Carrie doesn't get enough time to herself," Tim exclaimed.

"Carrie is *my* governess," Reggie answered him primly. "Maybe we could go in the Rav?"

"Why not!" Carrie took pity on Tim. "Does that suit you?" She gave him a lazy smile, wishing it was Royce McQuillan who had asked her to go riding.

"You can't get rid of this sweetheart for the day?" Tim only half joked.

"No, she can't," Reggie said, grinning and showing the wide space between her front teeth. "I'll be—" she snapped her fingers "—what's that word...?"

"Chaperone?" Tim asked sarcastically.

"That's it!" Reggie crowed. "Anyway, Carrie has a boyfriend at home."

"Have you?" Tim looked at Carrie with a twisted grin. "Why wouldn't you, you're so beautiful!"

"I bet they're going to get engaged," Reggie said. "Carrie is going to sell the pictures to *Woman's Day*."

Carrie stood up, laughing, looking around for the colourful matching sarong to tie around her waist. "Reggie's talking about a friend of the family. I believe she was offered twenty-five thousand dollars for wedding pictures."

"You think she'll accept?" Tim flashed the child a glance.

"You bet she will," said Reggie airily.

Both Carrie and Tim burst out laughing, which was the way Royce McQuillan found them. What a tableau! he thought. Innocent youth, carefree, snatching fun, yet it irritated him enormously.

Tim, who really needed ticking off, was looking at the very light-clad Carrie with a positively worshipful expression on his face; Carrie, all pale honey limbs and an exceptionally beautiful body apparently quite unselfconscious under that drooling regard; Reggie, sitting happily on a rock munching on a red apple.

Royce sat his bay stallion for a moment easing back on his frown before calling out to the young jackeroo. "Tim, aren't you supposed to be giving Lance a hand?"

Immediately Tim spun around, all respect. "Sorry, boss. I heard the girls splashing so I decided to come down and say hello."

"I'm sure they appreciated that," Royce clipped off. "Say goodbye now and get on with it. There's a whole lot more for you to do before sundown." He had taken it fairly easy on Tim knowing Tim was basically filling in time but the boy's little breaks were becoming too frequent. He would have a private word with him later on in the day.

"See you Saturday, then, Carrie?" Tim murmured swiftly, watching Royce McQuillan dismount.

"Better get going, Tim," Carrie said, reading the older man's body language. "I'll pick you up at two outside the bunkhouse."

"That'll be great!"

"So long, Tim!" Reggie called brightly. "We might take a nice picnic."

Picnic? Royce walked on, pretending not to hear. As Tim reached him he added a few more instructions, then he continued on to the spring, its dark green surface sparkling with tiny bubbles like the bubbles in champagne.

"How's it going?" he asked, watching Carrie stoop

gracefully to pick up a sarong which she tied native-fashion around her slender hips.

"Really, really good," Reggie said in a high sweet voice, looking more like a little boy than a girl in her serviceable T-shirt and shorts, but she was filling out, McQuillan thought with satisfaction. There was flesh on those little chicken bones. And she looked contented, eyes bright, a ready smile on her lips.

"How long has Tim been here?" he asked, avoiding sounding stern.

"Only a few minutes," Carrie supplied, trying to fathom why when she never felt the least bit self-conscious in her bathing suit in front of Tim she felt close to stark naked under Royce McQuillan's brilliant gaze. Not that he was looking at her in any sexual way. All in all the look was a mix of arrogance and irritation.

"He asked us out Saturday," Reggie supplied with enthusiasm.

"I don't believe it," he said.

"You'd better believe it." Reggie nodded her head owlishly. "It's true, isn't it, Carrie? I think he's fallen in love with her," she told Royce in an aside.

"Nonsense," said Carrie, not at all disconcerted by the child.

"Hold on, he isn't *available* Saturday." Royce bent his gaze on the child's face.

"That's awful," said Reggie. "He said he was."

"I know how disappointed you must be," Royce glanced briefly at Carrie who looked more than ever like a day lily. "Tim just occasionally forgets he's supposed to be here to *work*. He had last weekend in town."

"Gee, we were going on a picnic," Reggie told him dolefully.

"Okay so *I'll* take you," Royce said.

Reggie rushed at him, grasping him around the knees. "You promise?"

"Reggie, I'm a man of my word." He ruffled her curls.

Reggie gave a whoop of delight. "And I love you!" she yelled. "Don't you just love him, too?" Reggie turned her head to appeal to Carrie.

"Your father is a wonderful man," Carrie said sweetly, feeling her face flushing.

"Why thank you, Catrina," he drawled with just the faintest hint of mockery.

"I mean, everyone says it," she added.

"Let's all pray for a beautiful day." He let his eyes rest on her until she felt her knees buckle.

"So where are we going?" Reggie asked, clinging to his hand.

"I'll have to give that some heavy thought," he told the child. "If we make it a day trip we could take the helicopter and visit the rainforest. We'd have to leave the helicopter, of course. Set up the next leg of the trip."

"Oh, can't we, Royce?" Reggie sounded thrilled out of her mind at the offer. "I'll be so good. Carrie will love it."

"It sounds marvellous." Carrie, too, found herself responding with enthusiasm. "But what am I going to do about Tim?" She looked directly into Royce's sparkling jet eyes.

"I'll tell him," he said.

When Lindsey heard about the proposed trip to the rainforest she decided she wanted to go. "It will make a nice break in the monotony," she said as they lingered over coffee.

"If you're bored, my dear, you could always take a trip to Brisbane. You have friends there," her husband told her.

"It's no fun on my own." Lindsey regarded him coolly.
"They're all happily married. No one wants a woman on
her own. If you're young enough and attractive enough
you're seen as a threat. No, the rainforest will do fine."

"I'll have to check with Reggie," Royce McQuillan
said smoothly. "It's *her* trip."

"You can't be serious," Lindsey flared.

"Indeed, I am. You and Reggie aren't exactly on the
best of terms."

"In fact, my dear," Cameron McQuillan said mildly,
"You've given the child a rather bad time."

Lindsey blinked. "That's a bit much," she protested.
"Regina has been a lot more civil since Carrie arrived. I
scarcely ever hear her uttering her swearwords anymore."

"She might break out again if I tell her we're taking
extras," Royce said, swallowed his coffee hot and strong.
"Needless to say, Lyn, I'd love you to come along."

Reggie, when she did hear Lindsey wanted to come,
whipped out her worst word, so cross she scarcely heard
Carrie's remonstration. "She'll spoil everything," Reggie
fumed. "She always does. She'll want to talk to Royce all
the time. It's no good trying to get a word in. Why doesn't
he just tell her she can't come?"

Carrie swallowed. "I expect he's concerned about hurt-
ing your uncle Cam's feelings. After all, Lindsey is his
wife."

Reggie sank to the floor and buried her face in her
hands. "I knew it was too good to be true. I wish she'd
step on a taipan."

Carrie crouched down beside the child. "Oh, don't say
that, sweetheart," she shuddered. "You mustn't say things
like that. God is listening."

"He knows how nasty I am," Reggie said with a helpless shrug. "Can't you please ask Royce not to take her? He listens to you."

"I don't know that he will," Carrie groaned, not happy about Lindsey's coming along on the trip, either.

"He's very pleased with the way you take care of me. He told me. Anyway he doesn't even like Lindsey. Want to hear something? He and Gran begged Uncle Cam not to marry her. Uncle Cam should have listened. You should hear what Aunty Ina calls her, and they're supposed to be friends."

"No, thank you, Reggie. I don't want to know."

"Well, it's slut," Reggie muttered.

"How very unkind. You've been listening to far too much talk for a little girl." Carrie frowned.

"That's because they forget I'm there. I don't want her to come, Carrie. Please speak to Royce."

So Carrie waited that night for Royce McQuillan to go to his study, then she followed him.

"May I have a word?"

"Come in," he said briefly. "Shut the door. I suppose you could even lock it."

"Isn't that a bit drastic?" She glanced behind her.

"It's the only way to keep people out."

"Am I people?" she asked nervously.

"No, you're okay." He gave her just a glimpse of his beautiful smile. "Fire away."

Carrie slipped into a chair facing his massive partners desk. Directly behind him was a portrait of his grandfather, Sir Andrew McQuillan, a handsome stern-faced man with thick, silvered hair in stark contrast to the now familiar jet-black eyes. The artist had caught perfectly the aura of power and distinction.

"Reggie has asked me to beg you not to take Lindsey on our trip," Carrie began.

"Splendid!" He looked up from some paper in front of

him. "I don't just insult Lindsey, you know. I insult my uncle."

"I know. It's a difficult situation."

"My God, tell me about it!" he invited. "Problems and troubles. That's what my life's been up to date."

"You might solve a few things if you..."

"Show them the door?"

"I wasn't going to put it quite so bluntly."

He was silent for a while, staring at her. "I like you in white. White for the pure of heart."

"It's cool in the heat. Are you sure we're not going to get a storm?"

"Are you feeling in need of a bit of excitement?" he asked suavely.

"I'm just commenting on the heat of the night. The humidity is very high, as well."

"The tropics, Catrina." He stood up and flicked a switch that drove a five-bladed dark timber and brass fan. "Better?" He looked down at her. Her beautiful skin was matt and flawless. Hair and eyes shone. She looked the picture of youth, beauty and health. In fact she tore his sore heart.

"Thank you. So what do I tell her?"

"Tell her she's the one who spilt the beans," he said dryly, resuming his seat.

"She was excited, that's all. It was my own reaction."

"I'll have a word with Reggie," he told her.

"Don't you ever want her to call you daddy?" Carrie found herself asking wistfully.

"Royce is a good name," he answered crisply. "It's on my birth certificate. You're sure not backward in coming forward, are you?"

"I suppose not. I plunge right in. It's just that it seems a little..." She shrugged. "Reggie loves you so much. I'm certain letting her call you Royce is well intentioned, but daddy has to be one of the most beautiful words in the world.''

"Thank you for sharing that with me, Miss Russell," he mocked, "but you must respect *my* decision to allow Reggie to call me Royce.''

"I'm sorry." Carrie bit her lip.

"I trust you are. Whose idea was it for Jada to give Reggie drawing lessons?''

"Mine. You should see them together. They love it. I can't draw very well at all.''

"Surely you have enough talents. Like your music." He stared at her with his lancing eyes. "If you don't go to the piano soon you'll forget how to play.''

"The piano is all covered up.''

"What an excuse. I'll have the cover removed. If you're qualified to give advice, so am I. I'm sympathetic to your great disappointment, Catrina, but, we agreed, I thought, you can't brood on it overmuch. Try to let go of the pain. I'm genuinely very interested in hearing what you can do. Want to try playing something?''

"No," she said emphatically, backing off when faced with it.

"Okay," he said equably, "not tonight. You probably want to practise first.''

"I hate you." She looked at him and suddenly her great golden eyes blazed.

He sat back casually. "I can live with it. However, if you dare repeat it, I'll terminate your employment.''

"Would you?" Her anger evaporated.

"Not really. I value your services too highly. Now, Catrina, I have work to do. Tell Reggie, on condition she can keep her mouth shut, there'll be just the three of us.''

"You're saying you're going to tell Lindsey she can't come?''

"You're questioning I'm not game enough to try it?''

"No way!" Carrie stood up and smiled. "I figure you can handle just about anything."

Carrie was making her way along the quiet gallery when Lindsey emerged from her private sitting room to call her. "Can you spare me a minute of your precious time?"

It wasn't the friendliest greeting in the world but Carrie answered pleasantly. "Certainly, Mrs. McQuillan." She'd taken note of the fact Lindsey McQuillan preferred the formal address.

"Come in," Lindsey indicated with an abrupt movement of her hand Carrie should join her in the sitting room which was furnished with fine pieces taken from all over the house. If nothing else Lindsey enjoyed luxury, Carrie thought. She had never seen Lindsey in the same outfit twice. All of her clothes bore a top designer label. In the heat of this night she was wearing a deeply dipping short sapphire-coloured dress which enhanced her eyes, matching sandals on her feet. She could have worn it to the most chic party but she dressed day in, day out to dazzle. For a married woman, her judgement was seriously under question.

Carrie felt yet another stab of pity for her, wondering how and where Cameron McQuillan had met his wife and married her despite deep family misgivings. Reggie, who had heard far too much for a child, let alone one of her tender years, was a mine of information.

"I saw you follow Royce to his study," Lindsey said in an intense accusing voice, moving into an armchair and crossing her legs. "What was that all about?"

Carrie with the redhead's temper felt her teeth go on edge. "A private matter, Mrs. McQuillan, to do with Reggie."

"Don't you think you overdo running to Royce?" Lindsey's remarkable eyes flashed.

"I don't at all." Carrie managed to speak calmly. "I can't see how you can accuse me of that. What is it you *really* want to talk to me about, Mrs. McQuillan?" No sense in not getting to the point.

"Thank God you're not stupid!" Lindsey said. "I want to warn you not to go falling in love with Royce. I can't help thinking you're well on the way."

Carrie didn't even stop to think what she was saying. "It must be the norm around here," she said wryly. Causing Lindsey to sit high in her armchair.

Her mouth worked for a minute before she could speak. "I beg your pardon?" The expression on her face was of complete shock.

"Look, I don't want to upset you," Carrie said, *meaning* it, "but it's very obvious you're attracted to Royce yourself."

Lindsey sat staring at her. "What a colossal cheek! How dare you!" She was so startled her voice actually shook.

"I'm trying to be a friend to you," Carrie said quietly. "It's a sad situation."

"And none of your business," Lindsey cried sharply. "I remind you we're talking about *you.*"

"Oh, no, not *me.* I'm not your enemy here, Mrs. McQuillan," Carrie said. "And I don't allow women to attack me. You asked for it."

"And I got it in spades." Lindsey blinked.

"I'm sorry. I really am."

"You'll be sorrier if you ever try to come between Sharon and Royce," Lindsey warned, a curious, almost exultant expression on her face.

"You mean the *ex* Mrs. McQuillan?" Carrie pointed out.

"She's still very much in the picture." Lindsey laughed.

"I don't think everyone knows about that," Carrie answered mildly. "Certainly not Royce."

This conversation wasn't going at all as Lindsey intended. "My dear, there's *lots* you don't know," she said very coldly.

"I daresay there is. But I wouldn't care to hear it from someone like your friend Ina. I'd watch out for her if I were you." Carrie threw in a warning of her own.

Lindsey turned an odd colour. "What are you talking about?"

"Just a rumour. Be more careful, she's not to be trusted."

Lindsey took a deep shuddering breath, her anger momentarily abated. "Hang on, who's giving you all this information. Is it Gran? You're spending more and more time with her."

Carrie shook her head decisively. "Mrs. McQuillan doesn't *gossip*. She loves to tell me stories about the old days on the wilderness coast. I love to listen. It's a real insight into what must have been a unique way of life. She's a fascinating woman with many fascinating stories to tell. I enjoy her company and I've grown fond of Jada, too. She's so devoted to Mrs. McQuillan. It's lovely to see."

Lindsey's expression was cynical. "My dear, you don't think I've got the picture? You've done everything in your power to ingratiate yourself since you arrived here. You've even got poor old Cam eating out of your hand."

"Your husband is a very nice man, gentle and charming," Carrie pointed out.

"No he's *not*, he's a bastard," Lindsey burst out, her face working. "He's got *nothing* to offer me! I thought we were going to travel the world. I thought we were going to have a good time. Instead he can't bear to leave his bloody home. If that isn't pathetic, what is? God that man has a lot to answer for."

It was certainly a different point of view. "Surely you

can convince him you want a home of your own?'' Carrie challenged, feeling the other woman's inner rage. ''You'd feel so much better in different surroundings. Don't you want children?''

''No, I don't.'' Lindsey sat there, face white. ''Children were never on the agenda. I want a *life*.''

''Then you'd better move away from Maramba,'' Carrie suggested. ''I'd say right now.''

Lindsey was silent, absorbing Carrie's frank advice. ''Why am I letting you talk to me this way?'' she asked finally.

''I expect you need someone to confide in. I'm sympathetic to your plight.''

''Hell, yes.'' Lindsey stood up and stalked to the French doors. ''You're in love with him yourself. Don't bother denying it. We women can read one another like books.''

''Mrs. McQuillan, I'm keeping my head down,'' Carrie said. ''I'm here as Reggie's governess. I'm not about to empty my innermost thoughts into your ear. While we're on the subject of Reggie might I ask you not to fill her head with stories about evil spirits at the bottom of the home lagoon. She pretends to be so confident but she's only a little girl. It scares her. I can't begin to teach her to swim.''

''Oh, no, I just thought it was a way of keeping her away from the water,'' Lindsey apologised with huge difficulty. ''She's such a mad little devil. In fact she's a lot like her mother. Sharon is very unstable. If you ask me Sharon's a manic depressive. If she's not on some great high, she's in hell. The child's the same.''

''I don't accept that,'' Carrie answered flatly. ''Reggie has been neglected, starved of a mother's love.''

Lindsey gave her a bitter smile. ''So that's the plan? You're going to make yourself indispensable to Reggie so you can get Royce?''

"Looks like our little conversation is over," Carrie said, standing up. "I'm not a manipulative person. I'm not greedy or ruthless. I don't have a plan. I have a few demons to wrestle myself before I can even start making plans of my own. I can only tell you I'm not your enemy. Please don't treat me like one."

The trip to the rainforest—minus Lindsey—was a wonderful new experience for Carrie and Regina. Royce had organised a guide and he led them through part of one of the last great remaining rainforests of the world. Warm, humid, golden-green, the plant life was overwhelming in its profusion and diversity, the great trees with their crowns interlocking formed the forest canopy covered with other plants, mosses, ferns, orchids, elkhorns and staghorns on a massive scale. Ferns stood the size of trees while the wonderful ancient cycads dominated the lower levels. It was a very hot day when they started on the verge of the wet, but on the rainforest floor everything was quiet and calm. Thick woody vines lay all over the rainforest floor, or hung like gigantic ropes from the trees. Epiphytes heavily adorned the tree trunks or even bare rocks while beautiful posies of flowers, a phenomenon called cauliflory dotted the trunks of the forest giants, climbing a hundred feet or more.

At one point they had to come to a complete halt, Reggie hushed and excited, as a giant bird called a cassowary, black-feathered and flightless with brilliant blue and red colours on its head, neck and wattles, stalked out of the forest undergrowth. They all stood perfectly still, the guide in front, Royce standing protectively in front of Carrie and the child, his arms stretched back. The bird moved quietly, booming and rumbling, obviously looking for food. Five feet tall, heavy birds, cassowaries could be dangerous and were known to attack man if the nest was threatened. But there were innumerable wild fruits in the forest. The cassowary moved off, despite its size difficult to see against the great profusion of plants.

Afterward when Reggie grew tired Royce carried her back to the rainforest edge where butterflies in their thousands, a giant kaleidoscope of colour were swarming all over the massed stands of pink and purple lantana; lace wings, cruisers, birdwings, spotted triangles, the magnificent iridescent blue Ulysses with its huge wingspan. Here, too, in the sunlight they were able to appreciate the brilliant plumage of the birds, so difficult to see in the density of the rainforest branches.

It was a perfect day but that perfection wasn't to survive the night.

When they arrived back on Maramba, later afternoon, Royce was greeted by his overseer, who appeared to be waiting just for the purpose of telling him a charter plane had flown in that afternoon with Mrs. Sharon McQuillan as a passenger.

"Mummy?" Reggie asked in wonderment, her eyes round with surprise.

"She's got a bloody nerve!" Royce McQuillan muttered, shaking his head disbelievingly, his voice bitter.

"You're not going to fight, are you, Royce?" Reggie asked after such a happy day, on the verge of tears.

"No of course we're not, poppet." He recollected himself instantly. "Let's go and see what she wants."

"It can only mean trouble," he told Carrie, as Reggie made a beeline to get into the Jeep.

Carrie stood her ground, experiencing a whole jumble of perturbing emotions; panic, anxiety, an unwelcome rush of jealousy she couldn't fight down. Worst of all, she felt threatened. What were the consequences of their own

deepening relationship, very serious on her part and, she'd
hoped and believed, on his.

"It might be best if you and Reggie keep out of the way
until I can see what this is all about."

"You mean out of sight?" She wasn't certain how to
do it; wasn't certain she wanted to.

"Sharon didn't come to see Reggie," he said bluntly,
"hell, don't you think I want the child to have a loving
mother? Tragically that's not on."

Somehow they made it into the house without encoun-
tering anybody, Royce McQuillan instructing Carrie to
take Reggie upstairs.

She obeyed, shaky inside and absorbing the danger. She
wanted to stay near him. It was obvious he was deeply
disturbed as she was herself. What hold did this woman
have over him? She had seen him directing his men, noted
his easy bred-in-the-bone authority. He had no problem
being master of a great station, but he still had a problem
with his ex-wife.

Was it possible he still cared for her? Carrie agonised,
painfully aware of her own lack of worldliness. If he did,
how could she possibly cope with it? Sharon McQuillan
was a woman who damaged lives, but she was very sexy
with a lot of style. Also, and Carrie had seen it with her
own eyes, Sharon had not succeeded in breaking free of
her ex-husband. Were both of them left with feelings they
didn't want? Was it possible Royce McQuillan was out of
reach altogether?

Holding Reggie firmly by the hand, praying the child
wasn't going to get out of hand, they made the upper gallery where she saw Jada beckoning to her from the far
end.

"Your grandmother wants to see us, Reggie," Carrie
said, going toward the aboriginal woman.

"Gran doesn't like Mummy." Reggie spoke huskily, as though her throat was red raw.

"Everything will be all right, darling. Don't you worry," Carrie tried to reassure her. "Your mother and father are adults. They can talk in an adult way."

"You haven't heard my mummy when she's *mad!*" Reggie said, clutching Carrie's hand tighter. "She can screech like a cat. Maybe she wants to stay?"

"Would you *want* her to stay?" Carrie asked. Sharon was the child's mother, for all that.

"Gran said Mummy doesn't know how to behave," Reggie said as though that settled it.

"Gran didn't *tell* you that?"

"No, she was talking to Royce."

"You'll have to stop listening in to the adults' conversation, Reggie," Carrie warned. "Think of it as a little sin."

"No it's not," said Reggie. "It's not at all. It's my way of finding out what's going on." And in its way it was very effective.

Jada let them in to Louise McQuillan's bedroom. Carrie was quite familiar with the layout of the west wing having spent companionable time with the old lady. She had brought Reggie with her several times and Reggie had behaved. Carrie hoped that state of affairs was going to hold, especially as the old lady looked frailer than ever, almost diminished.

"Sharon is in the house," she announced, and the words came out like a sad wail.

"I'm sure everything is going to be all right, Mrs. McQuillan." Carrie went to the old lady and gently took her hand. "You're upsetting yourself for nothing."

The old lady gave a hollow laugh. "Difficult not to, my dear." She lay back on the pillows.

"I'll look after you, Gran." Reggie followed Carrie to

the bed, speaking amazingly soothingly for such a young child. "Maybe Mummy's come to be friends?"

Weak tears sprang into Louise McQuillan's eyes. "You're a good little girl, Reggie. Would you go with Jada for a minute while I speak to Catrina?"

"Sure, Gran." Reggie bent over and kissed the old lady's hand on the coverlet. "What do we do if she wants me back?"

"Would you want to go, Reggie?" Louise McQuillan asked very gently.

"I don't know. I don't think so," Reggie's voice trailed off. "Maybe just a holiday. But I don't want to be away for Christmas. I don't want to go anywhere without Carrie." She started to sound agitated.

"Come along, child." Jada took the little girl's hand, smiling down at her.

"I've got a nice drink for you. Let your gran talk to Carrie now."

Reggie went off willingly, walking with Jada into the adjoining sitting room.

Louise McQuillan waited until she heard their voices in the next room before she continued. "You haven't been with us that long, Catrina, but I feel I know you. I trust you. I know you're mindful of Reggie's welfare. I have to tell you I'm worried and I can't hide it. I don't know what Sharon's visit means, coming like it does out of the blue. Or worse, someone could be feeding her information. She picked her day. I'd like to think she felt compelled to see her child but we've all learned the hard way. My great fear is Sharon is going to try to use Reggie in some way."

"You mean as leverage, bargaining power?" Carrie asked, not really understanding at all.

"She's not above it," Louise McQuillan said. "I want you to stay close to Reggie. Protect her if you can. Protect her from what she might hear."

Carrie felt brave enough to risk it. "Is there something I don't know about, Mrs. McQuillan?" she asked simply. "Something that might help me do my job."

Louise moved her knotted hands. "Just be warned. Royce has a temper. He won't take too much without exploding. Sharon will do everything in her power to provoke him. She can't *let go* but she can never be allowed into this family again."

"But what about Reggie?" Carrie asked in concern. "Does her mother have *no* love in her heart for her?"

Louise bit her lip. "The awful truth is Sharon has never wanted Reggie from the moment she was born. She never loved or tended to her. Royce had to get in a nurse. Sharon was treated for postnatal depression though her doctor doubted she had the condition at all. I believe Reggie was an unwanted pregnancy. Poor little Reggie has had to pay the price."

Carrie looked at her in bewilderment. "But a woman so madly in love with her husband, bearing his child…" It was incomprehensible to Carrie.

"Maybe if she had looked like Sharon." Louise shredded a tissue. "Sharon was a striking little girl with her dark hair and those ice-blue eyes. Reggie will come into her own when she's older."

"Reggie is remarkably intelligent," Carrie said loyally.

"It might be better if she were just an ordinary little girl," Louise answered bleakly. "Reggie's a thinking child. She's been very badly hurt. Be there for her, Catrina. That's all I ask."

CHAPTER EIGHT

MRS. GAINSFORD served them a meal in Carrie's bedroom, her manner more subdued than ever but surprisingly kind. "I've made those noodles you like, Regina," she said gently, "and a chocolate pudding. I hope you enjoy. Chicken salad for you, Carrie, as it's too hot. Nice fresh rolls. A family dinner tonight, I understand." She didn't mention Sharon but they were all intensely aware of "A Situation."

After the housekeeper had gone Carrie wheeled the trolley out onto the verandah, pulling up chairs and encouraging Reggie to eat up her meal. She had lost all appetite herself but for the child's sake she pretended interest in her meal, which really was delicious, the fresh garden salad flavoured with a piquant Thai dressing. Though she expected to hear a knock on the door at any moment requesting Reggie come down to see her mother, none came. Even Reggie gave up expecting it, making no fuss about going off to bed, closing her eyes as though she wanted to escape the whole unhappy business.

After a stifling night, Carrie was aroused in the early hours by the wind. It gusted into her room at near gale force, lifting the sheer curtains so they danced with spectacular abandon, the edge of one catching an ornament and sending it crashing over.

"Damn and blast!" A little dizzy from the heat and humidity, Carrie pitched the pillow that had been tucked under her head out of the way and leapt out of bed, adrenaline pouring into her body. Now she could see the light-

162

ning that momentarily blinded her and bleached the world before disappearing into the walls of jungle. Hastily she closed one side of the French doors, catching the curtains back in their loops. Distant rumbles of thunder were swiftly coming closer.

After the trials of the evening why not a fierce storm? she thought a little desperately. A storm might clear the air but it could be dangerous. Not that she hadn't lived through many a bad electrical storm at home but she had never seen lightning like that. If her curtains were thrashing about wildly so would Reggie's. She didn't want the little girl awake and frightened. With the shutters secured inside the bedroom would be relatively calm and she had turned on the ceiling fan for coolness. The good thing was Reggie, childlike, could sleep through just about anything including morning calls to rouse her.

Without bothering to pull on her robe, Carrie took to the verandah rushing down its length to Reggie's room, starting back as hundreds of fruit bats who had been feeding on the mangoes, the bananas and the custard apples, flew screeching over the roof in their race for shelter. It did nothing to soothe her agitation. Her hand lifted to her throat as the crickets, the cicadas and the frogs joined in the general din. It all sounded barbarous, an assault on the senses. Lightning flashed again, then a great crack of thunder so loud she thought it might do permanent damage to her ears. Shudders ran up and down her spine. The force of the wind was whipping her long hair, making it sail around her. Her nightdress felt like it was going to be shredded to ribbons. The rain was coming down now. Huge drops that splattered. Even the rain was hot. She rushed for shelter, pitching headlong into someone emerging from Reggie's room...

For a moment he was as startled as she was, his heart

contracting before expanding, his arms locking around her, capturing her as if she were some wraith of the storm.

"Good God, what have I got here?" he murmured from a husky throat.

Such a question when no one absolutely no one else could have aroused such lavish arousal. She was just barely covered in the finest cotton, dressed up with little bits of ribbon and lace and tiny buttons that pressed into his chest. The nightdress was clinging to her body, scented with the nectar of her and the sharp blood-warm greenness of the rain. She didn't struggle. Indeed her bones seemed to turn to liquid so she was like silk in his arms. As they stood there, lightning blazed in the lacquer-black night, burning his downward view of her into his retina. Her breasts were barely masked by the feather-light fabric. They gleamed opalescent; the tips bruised a dark rose. He wanted to stoop and cup her breasts in his hands. He wanted to suckle the sweet budding nipples.

Catrina, he thought. My God, my heart!

Desire licked through his flesh; a frantic need for gratification. She was no sacrifice to his disturbed dangerous mood. He was in love with her. He had been from the moment he'd laid eyes on her. Everything leading him to that point in his life like a revelation. But there was danger for both of them in its driving force, the thought he couldn't stop. She was whispering to him, looking urgently toward the small figure of Reggie curled up sound asleep in her bed.

"I was going to close the shutters." Her breath came in little exhalations.

"My thought, too." Abruptly he released her, trying to beat back the desperation that was in him. "Why don't you move back onto the verandah while I do it? You'll have to change your nightdress anyway. It's damp."

He, on the other hand, was fully clothed. In fact he

hadn't gone to bed, too deeply disturbed by his ex-wife's visit and its implications for Regina.

Incredibly Sharon hadn't made an immediate request to see her child as almost any other mother in the world would have, saying she preferred to wait until morning to give Regina "a few early Christmas presents." She was, however, "absolutely ecstatic" to see him. A woman so ego-driven she couldn't see it was one of the great turn-offs of his life. Innocent little Reggie's birth had destroyed any tender feelings he might have had for Sharon though it took him eighteen months to find out for sure Reggie wasn't his.

Swiftly he closed the timber shutters leaving the French doors open for the heat. The verandahs were deep. Even in the worst of storms the full force of the rain didn't reach the central core of the house. Reggie was lost in her dreams. He hoped they were good.

His hand stretched out to take hers as he led Catrina back to her room. The spray from the rain, swirling a blue mist as the lightning lashed, enveloping them both, slicking their skin and wetting their clothes, but never cooling the waves of fire in the blood. They had barely reached Carrie's room before the force of his feelings overcame him. His arm cradled her back as he bent her over his arm.

"God, I want you!" he uttered, the soft moan edged with a trace of violence as passion and a self-imposed restraint warred within him. He lowered his head over hers, took her mouth, found it open and waiting, wet and tasting of rain. Her nightgown was plastered to her and he had the most powerful urge to ease it from her body. To hold her naked in his arms. He couldn't even hear the thunder that was cracking overhead so great was his own agitation. Just how much was a man supposed to take? To have this young woman under his roof. A young woman so good at communicating with his family, leading a troubled child with the gentlest of reins. To see her day in and day out. Dine with her at night, see her behind his eyelids as he finally closed his eyes for sleep.

As he withdrew his mouth momentarily to give her breath, something flickered on the periphery of his vision. In an instant he was alerted. Someone was moving along the verandah. A woman. He wasted no time. Now wasn't the moment for some shocking confrontation. With the tall curving fronds of the golden canes screening them he lifted Catrina clear off her feet and carried her back into her room.

"Go to bed!" he clipped off with so much urgency, Carrie found herself obeying. He sounded too remarkably sober for a seduction scene, a feat in itself after the tumultuous passion of his kiss. Even though she was all but soaked to the skin, she lay down on the extreme edge of the bed, watching him make short work of closing the other French door before shooting home the bolt.

It was beyond Carrie's understanding. A bizarre melodrama but despite that she trusted him with all her heart. Moments later with Royce standing well back in the dark recesses, a woman's figure appeared ghostlike outside Carrie's locked doors. It gave Carrie such a fright she uttered a strangled little cry in her throat that mercifully was lost in the turbulence of the night.

Sharon! Carrie had a moment of devastating revulsion.

She turned on her back, half closing her eyes and pretending sleep. The room turned luminous as another bolt of lightning zigzagged down the sky. Sharon stared in. Incredibly the doors rocked back and forth as she attempted to open them, but they held. When Carrie turned to look again, Sharon was gone.

Immediately Carrie dashed up, her body shaking, pulling the sheer curtains out of their loops and across the French doors. This was a first in her life.

"Is it possible your wife thought she was going to find you in my bed?" she demanded of the tall figure who moved out of the shadows to be near her.

"My *ex*-wife," he corrected, then inexplicably began to laugh, holding it in before it became a shout. "You have to hand it to that woman for sheer cheek!"

"No way is she *normal*," Carrie breathed. "She didn't even want to see her own daughter. Would you like to try explaining all this?"

"Catrina, I haven't got the time," he mocked, "and it would drive me crazy."

"So we wait until she comes to the other door?"

He shook his head. "I hope you had the sense to lock up."

"Actually I did on account of her."

He nodded as if he understood exactly. "The time has passed for any reasonable talk with Sharon. I'm at the point of throwing her out."

"She's brought you a lot of misery, hasn't she?"

"Yes, but it's Reggie who has suffered the most." His voice was bleak.

"So what do we do now?" Carrie asked very quietly.

"I know what I'd like to do," he replied with black humour. "Take that nightgown off you and towel you dry."

She was mute for a moment, racked by little ripples that multiplied. "I'm not a child."

"You're telling me?" His low laugh was a shade harsh. "Failing that, I think I should pour myself a stiff drink."

"Well, I don't have one to offer you." Carrie shrugged helplessly. "Just as well. I might be persuaded to have one myself. But I will get out of this nightgown." She began to pad across the room, brought to a gasping halt as something pierced her foot. "Oh, no!"

"What is it?" he questioned, in his frustration a little fierce.

"I've cut my foot."

"How the devil could you do that?" He sounded concerned but very restless.

"The curtain knocked over an ornament. I'm sorry."

"That's okay, I'll take it out of your wages." Again a low laugh as though humour could reduce the tremendous electric charge between them. "Here, come into the bathroom." He found her bare shoulder, couldn't resist palming it.

"I might get blood on the rug," she warned. The rug was superb. Persian.

"Okay, so I carry you." He swooped and lifted her, kissing her a little roughly but oh so sweetly on the mouth.

"I'm getting accustomed to this, Royce McQuillan," she said in a hushed voice. "Be warned."

"Maybe it's me who's thinking you'll never get away from me," he answered.

Inside the spacious en suite he closed the door first before turning on the light. He deposited her on the marble bench, before gently taking hold of her foot. "This is what comes of running about in bare feet." He examined the soft area to the side of her instep. "Damn there's a tiny fragment still in it. You're not chilled, are you?" He dared a brief glance at her, desire still lashing at him.

"You're joking. I'm steaming." She gave a little laugh, reaching out for a hand towel, then patting her face and throat dry. "You're even wetter than I am." Her voice shook a little as her own feelings crested. His hair gleamed blue-black in the bright light, curling into damp waves and curls. His skin had the perfect polish of bronze. The soft shirt he had worn at dinner was dyed a deeper blue by the rain. He had undone a couple of buttons and pulled the wet collar back. She could see his muscular chest, the fine whorls of dark hair that lightly matted it. Not only the cut on her foot was throbbing. Her whole body was. The two of them sealed off in this quiet room.

"That's what comes of making love in the rain," he answered her as he walked away to the wall cabinet where he found cotton wool, antiseptic and some bandaids. "Your feet are as beautiful as your hands," he remarked as he went about tending the wound.

"I've been hearing that since I was two days old." She smiled.

"Aren't *you* lucky?"

"You can't really believe that?" She sought his brilliant eyes, her heart beating madly.

"I do." He answered as though it mattered a great deal to him. "I can see into the future, Catrina, and my vision of you is good."

"Do you believe in destiny?" she asked, her voice very soft.

"I surely do." He opened up. "It was my parents' destiny to die together in a plane crash. It was my destiny to marry Sharon and later divorce her. Gran keeps telling me fate is going to step in again, this time with the right woman. The woman who will put me under her spell from the moment I lay eyes on her."

Look at me. Look at me, Carrie begged silently. She had given him her heart. She couldn't take it back.

"Do you know her name?" she asked, her voice so faint she wondered if she had spoken at all.

"Suzanne." He plucked a name from the top of his head, his smile teasing.

"Really?" She searched his face with her great golden eyes, seeing the sparkle of humour.

"We can't stay here, Catrina, you know that." His senses were swimming with her nearness and the sight of her lovely body, much too lightly veiled. Her soft heavy hair was falling loosely, radiantly all around her shoulders, drying fast in the heat, her long legs naked, the skirt of her nightgown rucked up to her fine-boned knees. She looked sexy beyond belief, yet so young and innocent.

"Have you ever had a lover?" he found himself asking, his voice dropping in pitch.

She closed her eyes thinking if she kept them open he couldn't fail to see she was hopelessly, madly in love with him. "No," she answered truthfully. *I thought I'd been made love to but I've since learned I was wrong about that.* She opened her eyes again and stared back at him. "You make me sad, Royce McQuillan."

"I don't believe that. I can't." His fingers pressed gently on the pulse in her throat.

"Then why do you twist my heart?"

The admission made his senses soar. "Do I?" He was barely aware he moved, yet his hand reached out to caress her breast, pushing aside the low neck of her nightgown to find her seductive silky flesh. "Carrie, what am I doing?" he groaned. He was like a man split in two. One part of him wanted to let her go back to her virginal bed, the other thought there was no possible way he could let her.

She was luring him on, her hands reaching out to clutch his shoulders as he stroked her breast, her head tipped back, her back arching at the pleasure his hands were giving her.

"You are so beautiful!" He heard his own voice purr into her ear as his mouth began to track across her face, covering it with kisses...her throat...the upper swell of her breasts. He couldn't get enough of her.

She gasped when his mouth found her erect nipple, her body for a moment going rigid with that deep inhalation. He lifted his head, trying to contain himself to the point he was sure of her reactions but she cried out softly,

"Please don't stop!" Sensation after sensation was flashing down her spine, the pleasure so intense it was almost a pain too great to bear.

"I can't do this," he said after fevered minutes, even as he lifted her, crushing her in his arms. "I can't do it. Stop me." It was a cry of anguish torn from his lips. The very air vibrated around them, thrumming with shocked sexual pleasure and his violent arousal. She had to stop him. Before it was too late.

It seemed an eternity before Carrie could respond. Her every desire, her every need, her every want was for him. His hands were gripping her hips as she clung to him, his long fingers splayed toward the apex of her body that was contracting sharply in the throes of intense physical excitement.

"I'm sorry...sorry..." Her knees were almost buckling under her but she somehow managed to fall back against the door.

"God, what have you got to be sorry about," he muttered through white clenched teeth. "I'm acting like a man possessed." He raked his hand through his hair.

"I offered myself to you." Carrie took her share of responsibility for the explosive loss of control.

"And I'm going to take you, Catrina," he promised harshly, "but it's going to be the right place and the right time. I couldn't bear it if you came to hate me."

Her mind reeled at the very thought. Hate him? She loved him. Nothing to be done about it. "How could you say such a thing? You've changed my whole existence."

"Complicated it, too." His striking face was sombre. "There are things I haven't told you, Catrina. Information I've denied you. But I've felt like a man caged."

"Then tell me now." Her face radiated an intense urge to help.

"Not *now*." His smile twisted. "I can't be with you

like this. My whole mind and body is focused on making love to you. But I couldn't bear to trap you. It's going to be a bad day ahead. I feel it like a black reality—Sharon is a sick unstable woman. For years now my whole experience of her has been either elation or depression. Whatever happens, I don't want you to leave. Promise me?" He touched her cheek.

"Nothing easier." She stared up into his brilliant eyes. "I won't."

"I'll hold you to that." He smiled grimly, then reached past her to open the door.

"Is Mummy going to want to see me this morning?" Reggie asked, wringing Carrie's heart. She was laying out the child's clothes. The best outfit she could find. Good quality but dull. Carrie determined on a trip into town in the near future where she could buy the little girl some of the latest gear for children. Bright colours, bright patterns. There were some marvellous labels for kids. She would have Reggie's hair cut while she was at it. Reggie truly did have great hair but it fell into the fairly unmanageable category being thick and extra crinkly-curly. Both her mother and father had very dark hair, Royce McQuillan's blue-black, Sharon's a deep sable. Reggie's was pretty much nondescript, which was unusual. But she could change that when she was much older with the use of colour. Reggie was clever and funny, often hilarious, and Carrie had grown very fond of her. "Let's go downstairs and see." Carrie had come to her decision. "The two of us can't hide away up here. What do you say?"

Reggie pulled the blouse over her head and grinned. "Suits me. I haven't seen Mummy in ages."

"So we're going to show her what a debonair little girl you can be?"

"What's debonair?" asked Reggie.

"It means you have very charming manners and you're cheerful."

"That's me."

After the storm of the night before, it was a brilliant day outside, the sun slanting through the front door into the lobby. Holding Reggie's hand, Carrie made her way down to the informal dining room where she found Sharon and Lindsey seated together. Both looked up, their faces cold and without welcome.

"Good morning." Carrie spoke pleasantly, expecting Reggie to let go of her hand and rush toward her mother.

It didn't happen. Reggie continued to cling to her side and instead of holding out her arms, Sharon McQuillan addressed Carrie.

"So, the new governess, so beautiful and so talented! You never had the guts to admit who you were."

It was quite a frontal attack but Carrie didn't waver. "I'm sorry, you confuse me, Mrs. McQuillan. You speak as though I'd committed a crime?"

"Well, haven't you? Running after Royce. Where the hell was he last night?"

"I suggest you ask him," Carrie answered calmly. "I'll go away. I thought you might want to speak to your daughter?"

"No, don't go away," Sharon suddenly thundered, not able to hold back her jealousy and anger. "My child doesn't need a governess. I'm here to take her away."

"Sharon?" Lindsey flung the other woman a startled glance.

"You keep out of this, Lyn," Sharon warned. "This is *me*, remember. I'm awake to you. I just use you when I need information."

Lindsey stood up. "Really? I don't have to listen to this."

"Then clear off."

So much for mother love. So much for making the decision to come downstairs. "I'll bring Reggie back at another time," Carrie volunteered.

"Oooooooh, Reggie! What sort of name is that?" Sharon shouted.

"It's *my* name," Reggie answered with more than a touch of her old belligerence, surveying her mother's thin, glamorous figure, dressed in a pink silk shirt and matching narrow-legged trousers. "Aren't you happy to see me at all?"

"And what exactly is *your* greeting?" Sharon countered fiercely. "You have no manners at all. Come here and kiss me."

"I don't want to." Reggie shuffled her feet, a child trying to protect herself from further abuse.

"Reggie hasn't had her breakfast, Mrs. McQuillan," Carrie said, thinking it very necessary to get the little girl away. "I'll take her to the kitchen."

"And who the bloody hell are you?" Sharon asked coldly.

"She's my governess," Reggie shouted. "I love her and you give me the creeps."

Immediately Sharon was on her feet, rushing toward her daughter as though she intended to smack her, but before she could even make it halfway Royce McQuillan's menacing voice brought her up short.

"Cool it, Sharon, for God's sake!" He strode into the room, a tall daunting figure dressed in his everyday working gear of bush shirt, bandana, silver-buckled belt laced into jeans, the cattleman's elastic-sided riding boots on his feet. "Catrina—" he shot a piercing look at her "—take Reggie to the kitchen if she hadn't had her breakfast."

"I'm going." Lindsey flashed past him. "There's no place for me."

"Not any longer, Lyn," Royce McQuillan clipped off. "My family has received no loyalty from you."

"I never knew she was so mean," Lindsey cried, pointing a finger at Sharon. "She's mean, mean, mean. I've never known anyone so locked in on themselves."

"Let's go, Reggie," Carrie said to the little girl quietly, disturbed that the child was cowering against her. It wasn't her spunky little Reggie.

"Come on, sweetheart."

"How lucky you are to have this wonderful young woman as a governess, Royce," Sharon cried. "Have you had her in your bed yet?"

Carrie fled, keeping her hands over the little girl's ears until they were well out of earshot. Inside the kitchen she had to take a deep breath to steady herself. "It's all right, Reggie."

No response at all from Reggie but she continued to hold tightly to Carrie's hand. "Come on, love, let's make a smoothie," Carrie suggested, her voice as soft as velvet.

"I'm ashamed of my mother," Reggie said, suddenly responding to Carrie's stroking her head. "Isn't she awful?"

Perfectly odious, Carrie thought, but she couldn't possibly say. "She's angry about something, Reggie. Anger makes people out of tune with the world."

"I hope I don't have to go and live with her."

"I'm sure your father won't allow anything you don't want, Reggie." Carrie rubbed the little fingers between her own. Good fingers, very nimble. What had happened to her couldn't stand in the way of her helping others. She could teach Reggie to play. It could make the little girl very happy.

They were standing at the blender when Mrs. Gainsford hurried back into the kitchen. "My goodness!" She turned a panic-stricken face to them, chewing hard on her lip. It was obvious she was about to say more but Carrie signalled her with a shake of her head not to. "It's a pawpaw smoothie this morning, Mrs. Gainsford," she tried to speak normally. "This one is perfect. It looks like you've just picked it."

"I did, dear. It survived the storm. It's the bats that are the problem. We have to keep the fruit covered." The housekeeper hurried over, smiling at Reggie. "What about a scoop of ice cream in it this morning?" Her voice was as gentle as either Carrie or the child had heard it.

"Thank you, Mrs. Gainsford," Reggie said.

"Carrie, I left a basket of fresh eggs on the chinese table in the hall." Mrs. Gainsford turned her head. "Would you mind getting them for me, dear?"

"No problem." Carrie could see the housekeeper was deeply embarrassed and unwilling to venture outside her own domain. "I'll be back in a moment, Reggie."

"I'll look after her," Mrs. Gainsford said, going to the refrigerator. "Coconut or caramel ice cream, Regina?"

Very quietly Carrie made her way outside, hearing Sharon cry out, "I don't care what you think... You're the big man. So powerful! But this is one time you don't have any power over me because Regina isn't yours. *She's not your child!*"

In the ringing silence that followed Carrie felt too paralysed to move away.

"Watch out for me, Sharon," Royce McQuillan said in a voice so deadly Carrie came out of her stupor.

She found herself rushing down the corridor to the dining room trying to hold to her promise to Louise McQuillan to keep the family safe. She could hear Sharon babbling on almost incoherently, as she burst into the room.

"What are you trying to do, Mrs. McQuillan?" Carrie

cried. "Reggie might hear you. I tell you you'll break her heart."

"You have to leave here, Sharon," Royce McQuillan said. "That means today. I sure don't know what your real reason for coming here was."

That was too much for Sharon. She burst out laughing. "Why to check out your little girlfriend, darling. Lyn told me she'd fallen in love with you just like the others."

"Did she tell you I've fallen in love with Catrina?" he rasped. "Of course not. Neither of you would want to believe it. But I've finally found out about love. It took a while."

Sharon blanched. "You just want her because she's young and beautiful. It will wear off, I promise."

Whatever Royce intended to say it was forestalled by Mrs. Gainsford's shout.

"Regina!" she cried.

Only she had seen the little girl race through the front door, moaning to herself at what she had heard.

The housekeeper cried out again in a blind panic, consumed by guilt for having turned her back for a minute, only this time all three adults had converged on the lobby, Royce demanding of the woman what was going on.

Carrie knew. She couldn't explain how she knew. But she knew. "The lagoon." She flung a glance of such anxiety at Royce he took to his heels with Carrie racing after him, fear lending her wings.

They both looked on in total anguish as the child ran headlong down the slope, not stumbling as they desperately hoped, but making swiftly, surely for the glittering emerald waters of the lagoon.

"Reggie!" Royce McQuillan shouted with the full force of his lungs. "Stop. Reggie, stop." His face contorted with dread.

But the little girl ran on, plunging into the lake and disappearing instantly from view.

"Reggie!" Carrie screamed in an agony. This couldn't be happening. This was anyone's nightmare.

Royce with his galvanic burst of speed far outstripped her so she was able to watch him dive into the lagoon where he, too, disappeared as the sparkling waters of the lagoon closed over him.

Carrie ran on desperately, propelled without incident across the thick grass, still soggy from the storm. When she reached the water she fell into it, surprised at its depth, then dived. Crystal-clear on top, beneath was terrifyingly murky sediment rising from the bottom now that three bodies were in the water. She shot to the surface to take a breath, preparing to dive again only Royce rose from the middle of the lagoon with the child in his arms.

"Oh, thank God!" the words were ripped from her throat. Frantically Carrie swam toward them but he urged her back. "Get out of the water, Carrie," he called. "Get a blanket."

Somehow Jada was there, spreading a rug on the grass as Royce emerged with the child and immediately began to put his training into practice. Big stations were life and death places. It wasn't the first time he'd been on hand at a near drowning. There was no sign of Sharon. Mrs. Gainsford and Lindsey huddled together a distance away, both of them looking white and shocked, overcome by the drama.

While they all prayed, Royce started CPR, continuing until Reggie began to splutter and retch up lagoon water.

Carrie was on her knees beside the child, tears pouring down her cheeks, whispering over and over, "Reggie!" She thought she had endured agony with the loss of her career yet here was a little girl so damaged by adult cruelty she had given up on life. It put everything into perspective.

Racing down the slope came Royce's overseer, with two of the stockman and the young jackeroo, Tim Barton. All of them looked deeply shocked.

"God, Royce!" the overseer spoke. "Will we get a doctor?"

"She's all right now. I don't think she needs one." Royce turned his head to speak to them. "She wasn't in the water long but I'll get her up to the house and tucked into bed." He rose with the little girl in his arms, his handsome face showing all the signs of a profound anger and distress. "Carrie, get that rug around you." He turned his head, his eyes whipping over her.

Tim moved swiftly, settling the rug Jada passed him around Carrie's shoulders. She was paper-white with shock. Tim felt helpless. What had gone on here this morning? They all knew the ex-wife, Sharon, was on the station. For a beautiful woman, and Tim had met Sharon McQuillan twice in his life, there wasn't one person he knew who liked her, including his own father. More important, where was the mother now? Tim looked around. No sign of her. Why wasn't she holding her child? Why wasn't she crying as Carrie was? Nothing made sense to Tim. He looked on with mingled horror and fascination. This was one dysfunctional family! For all he admired the coolest dude he had ever met in his life. Royce McQuillan.

CHAPTER NINE

IT TOOK weeks for Reggie to recover from her ordeal. Years later with Reggie, happy and confident, performing brilliantly both academically and with her music studies, both Carrie and Royce considered the healing began with the piano lessons. The cover of the Steinway had come off and Carrie began to teach the little girl to play. Carrie wasn't looking for big results. This was therapy; an all-out effort to divert Reggie's mind from her sad thoughts. What Carrie hadn't expected was for Reggie to take to the keyboard like a duck takes to water, so by Christmas of that momentous year Reggie was eagerly looking forward to her lessons which she had twice a day to make progress swift.

Without slowing down to identify notation—that could come later—Carrie played little pieces, letting the child watch her hands. As a crash course it had big results. More satisfying to Carrie was the way Reggie showed every sign of being a "true" musician, wrapping herself in an armchair every time Carrie sat down to play, her small face intent and filled with delight. Their music became a marvellous common ground. Indeed Carrie's playing caused family spirits to soar. Even the workers around the homestead found it difficult not to stop work and listen.

As for Sharon, ashen-faced and badly shaken, she had flown out of Maramba the same afternoon as "Reggie's dip," which was the way the family, including Reggie, referred to it. The whole incident of necessity had to be played down. But before departing Sharon had emptied out all her own bitter resentments telling them all near hysterically, she didn't blame herself in the least for what had happened. She felt no responsibility for what Reggie had overheard. The child was an inveterate eavesdropper, picking up things she was never intended to hear. Redemption for Sharon may have lain in acceptance and remorse. Sharon chose the stony path of denial. Whatever transpired between Royce and his ex-wife, Carrie never did find out. All she did learn was Sharon had given up all claim to her child. There was no place in Sharon's busy life for Reggie. Her birth had been "a terrible accident." As far as Sharon was concerned, Reggie could continue to be brought up as a McQuillan. No one was going to hear the story from her. She had a reputation to guard after all. Royce swore she actually said that. Sharon had no sense of irony.

The greatest hurdle lay in Royce's explaining to Reggie just how life was, and the reasons he had kept so much from her, even allowing for her tender years. Royce was able to do this during a quiet discussion with the disturbed little girl, who had all but disappeared behind a fortress in an effort to protect herself. Nevertheless he managed to convince her she was his little girl "by choice." So he wasn't her birth father? They both had to accept that. But in every other respect she was. She was his daughter. He loved her. He wanted her. He would have had a huge problem with her going away with her mother.

As the weeks went by Reggie, mature beyond her years, came within reaching distance of acceptance. She was Regina McQuillan. Maramba was her home. Royce was her dad. She even began to call him that, tentatively at first then it became second nature. Carrie, it became abundantly clear, was very important in the scheme of things. Reggie looked to her for guidance, support and unstinting affection.

At the dawn of Christmas morning, just as they planned, Royce and Carrie took the horses and rode out to the open savannah that stretched away in all directions. This was private time for themselves. Time they desperately needed as their hunger for each other was profound. The homestead was full of Royce's relatives and more were expected to fly in later on in the morning. The extended McQuillan family always made a big thing of Christmas, coming back to the ancestral home for the celebration. This year Cameron and Lindsey would be missing from the festivities. They were currently in Europe enjoying an extended holiday. The matriach, Louise McQuillan who was feeling so much better these days with many burdens off her mind was greatly looking forward to a week long of family. All everyone wanted was for the rain to hold off. This was the start of the Wet. The wild bush heralded it by putting on a phenomenal floral display.

For some miles Royce and Carrie rode over dense wild green herbage scattered with countless little mauve and violet wildflowers. Parrots flashed by in their legions, their colours more brilliant than precious jewels, landing a distance ahead to feed on the abundant seeds and the sea of grasses whose multitude of greens changed shades with the direction of the dawn wind. The peace of the morning was magical. Across the vast open valley sleek Brahmins stood belly-high in the vivid green grasses, turning their heads slowly at their presence. The big muster involving all hands was over in readiness for the Wet. The cattle had been brought in from all points of the station.

On the return ride they came to a curving lagoon where the air was heavy with the scent of wild passionfruit. Prolific vines moored an old fence that had once been part of a holding yard, the globular fruit gleaming a rich purple in the sunlight.

"I want to show you something." Royce turned his head to speak to Carrie, a kind of urgency in his voice.

"We can dismount over there by the fig." He pointed to a massive tree with soaring flying buttresses.

Ducks and black swans in among the pink waterlilies on the sparkling sheet of water, the lilies held their heads high above the water. Some were delicately flushed with red. It gave Carrie a near mystical experience as pleasure flooded through her. She slipped down into Royce's waiting arms. This could only happen once in a lifetime, she thought. If at all. Every time he looked at her it was like actual physical contact. When he did touch her, her whole body sang. It was as if she had shed an outer layer of skin, revealing another all satiny new, infinitely susceptible to sensation. She had never felt voluptuous in her life. Now she revelled in her own skin. And all because of this man.

He bent his head to kiss her until she was shaking in his arms. "Last night the urge to come to you was so bad I spent most of it pacing the floor," he confessed. "I love you, Catrina. No one else will do," he proclaimed, his brilliant eyes holding hers.

"So there *is* such a thing as perfect love?" she whispered, her arms locking around his neck.

"Don't let anyone tell you any different," he answered, enchanted by her response. "You've changed my life. You *are* my life. What I can't take is not being your lover." He reached into the breast pocket of his shirt, pulling out a small box. He looked down into her face as a man looks at a woman he loves and wants. "This says *marry me*."

"Does it?" Carrie heard her voice quiver before she started to cry.

"Darling!" He gathered her to him, rocking her gently in his arms. "You mustn't do that. I want to make you *happy*."

"But you do!" Carrie dashed the emotional tears from her eyes. "I love you with all my heart."

"So open the box," he urged, his deep voice indulgent.

''I can't wait to hear what you think. I had the jeweller send me designs. I specified the stones. This is the result.''

Carrie opened the box, releasing a little gasp. ''I'm dreaming!''

''No you're not,'' he said vibrantly, the radiance of her expression taking his breath away.

''It's so beautiful, Royce. So precious.'' She stared up at him with huge golden eyes.

''It's *exactly* the ring for you.'' He took her left hand, kissed it, then slid home her engagement ring. It was of exquisite design, featuring a superb central stone, the famous Argyle cognac coloured diamond from Western Australia, flanked by glittering ice white pave set diamonds in a white-gold band. It was a very beautiful, valuable ring. ''The cognac diamond, beautiful as it is, is no match for your eyes,'' he told her, catching their glitter.

''Oh, Royce!'' She was consumed by a euphoria that had her hiding her head against his chest. ''Thank you. Thank you. I love it. I love *you*.''

He let her sob for a full minute before laughter and a wonderful warmth got the better of him.

''Catrina, sweetheart!'' He grasped a handful of her hair, making her look up.

''Don't you know women cry when they're ecstatic?'' she asked him. ''It's almost the rule.''

His low laugh was full of an answering love and a certain exultance. ''I can just picture you when our son is born.''

''Oh, yes!'' Carrie breathed, throwing up her arms to the cloudless blue heavens in one graceful sweep. ''How is it possible to love someone so much?'' she marvelled.

His response was thrilling and immediate. ''I'll show you when we're curled up in bed,'' he promised tenderly.

Like an omen, a breeze sprang up from nowhere. It shook out the flowering gums that grew near the lagoon, scattering them with golden blossom that settled on their hair and their shoulders. Exactly like confetti.

TO HAVE AND TO HOLD

Marriages meant to last!

They've already said "I do," but what happens
when their promise to love, honor and cherish
is put to the test?

Emotions run high as husbands and wives
discover how precious—and fragile—
their wedding vows are....
Will true love keep them together—forever?

Look out in Harlequin Romance® for:

HUSBAND FOR A YEAR
Rebecca Winters (August, #3665)

THE MARRIAGE TEST
Barbara McMahon (September, #3669)

HIS TROPHY WIFE
Leigh Michaels (October, #3672)

THE WEDDING DEAL
Janelle Denison (November, #3678)

PART-TIME MARRIAGE
Jessica Steele (December, #3680)

Available wherever Harlequin books are sold.

HARLEQUIN®

Makes any time special ®

Visit us at www.eHarlequin.com   HRTHATHR

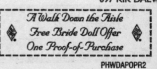

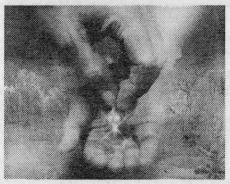

$\mathcal{H}$ugh Blake,
soon to become stepfather to
the Maitland clan, has produced three
high-performing offspring of his own. But
at the rate they're going, they're never going to
make him a grandpa!

There's *Suzanne*, a work-obsessed CEO whose Christmas spirit
could use a little topping up....

And *Thomas*, a lawyer whose ability to hold on to the woman
he loves is evaporating by the minute....

And *Diane*, a teacher so dedicated to her teenage students she
hasn't noticed she's put her own life on hold.

But there's a Christmas wake-up call in store
for the Blake siblings. Love *and* Christmas miracles
are in store for all three!

Maitland Maternity Christmas

A collection from three of Harlequin's favorite authors

Muriel Jensen
Judy Christenberry
&Tina Leonard

Look for it in November 2001.

Visit us at www.eHarlequin.com

PHMMC

Harlequin Romance ®

EXTRA!!! The Times EXTRA!!!

Runaway Bride Seeks Affair To Remember!

Do you like stories that get
up close and personal?

Do you long to be loved *truly, madly, deeply?*

Ever wondered what Harry *really* thought of Sally?

If you're looking for emotionally intense, tantalizingly tender love stories, stop searching and start reading:

LIZ FIELDING
JESSICA HART
RENEE ROSZEL
SOPHIE WESTON

They're fresh, flirty and feel-good.

Look out for their latest novels,
coming soon to Harlequin Romance®.